THE DUNDOODLE MYSTERIES

THE CHOCOLATE FACTORY GHOST

DAVID O'CONNELL

ILLUSTRATED
BY
CLAIRE POWELL

BLOOMSBURY

LONDON   OXFORD   NEW YORK   NEW DELHI   SYDNEY

BLOOMSBURY CHILDREN'S BOOKS
Bloomsbury Publishing Plc
50 Bedford Square, London, WC1B 3DP, UK

BLOOMSBURY, BLOOMSBURY CHILDREN'S BOOKS and the
Diana logo are trademarks of Bloomsbury Publishing Plc

First published in Great Britain in 2018 by Bloomsbury Publishing Plc

A catalogue record for this book is available from the British Library

ISBN: PB: 978-1-4088-8706-6; eBook: 978-1-4088-8705-9

2 4 6 8 10 9 7 5 3 1

Typeset by RefineCatch Limited, Bungay, Suffolk

Printed and bound in Great Britain by CPI Group (UK) Ltd,
Croydon CR0 4YY

To find out more about our authors and books visit www.bloomsbury.com
and sign up for our newsletters

For Dad, whose mountaineering exploits introduced me at a young age to the Highlands and Islands, and the magic of its landscape.

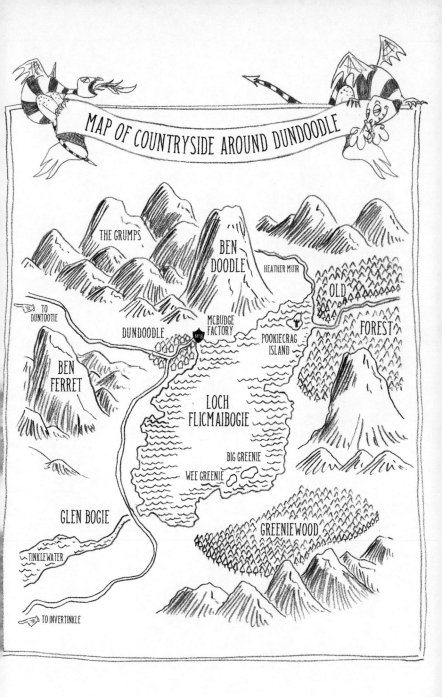

Archie stared up at the portrait of the old man. It had winked at him, hadn't it? He was sure of it. No, he must be imagining things. This spooky old house was playing tricks with his mind.

He was sitting in the very grand library of the very grand Honeystone Hall, surrounded by books – how could anyone own so *many* books? – and ancient, rickety and *very* dusty furniture. Were all the cobwebs real or were they specially delivered by the We'll-Make-Your-Home-Look-Creepy Company? Mum sat in the chair next to him, fidgeting like she had spiders dancing in her underwear and too preoccupied to pay any attention to misbehaving artwork. Had the portrait winked at him again? It hadn't. Had it? It HAD! It even grinned a little. This place was seriously WEIRD.

He dragged his eyes away from the painting which hung above the very grand fireplace.

'What are we *doing* here?' he whispered for the hundredth time.

'I don't *know*,' Mum whispered back. She gave the sparrow-like man shuffling papers, who sat in front of them, a sharp look.

'Can we get on with … *things*, Mr Tatters?' she said. 'We've come all the way from Invertinkle.'

'Of course, of course, dear lady,' said the lawyer amiably. 'Some of the details of this … *situation* are unusual. I was just checking a few particulars, but now we can proceed.' He cleared his throat dramatically.

'Archie McBudge,' said Mr Tatters, peering at the boy through a pair of grubby spectacles. 'You are a very fortunate young man. Very fortunate *indeed*. Great things lie in store for you.'

Archie had never thought he was destined for Great Things. A few Medium-Sized Things perhaps. 'Medium-sized' always sounded manageable. Great Things sounded like a *lot* of responsibility and he wasn't the ambitious type.

'Really?' was all he could say. *What was going on?*

'Whilst we mourn the recent *tragic* loss of your

great-uncle, Archibald McBudge ...' said Mr Tatters, pointing a bony finger towards the painting – *the* painting! He had a *Great-Uncle Archibald?* '... owner of McBudge's Fudge and Confectionery Company, and a dear, personal friend of mine ...' Archie's jaw dropped. McBudge's Fudge! He'd never even known Great-Uncle Archibald existed, but everyone knew McBudge's Fudge. It was the softest, sweetest-tasting, melt-in-the-mouthiest, fudgiest fudge you could buy. The best in the world. Archie had always been pleased he shared his name with a company that made something so famously tasty, but he'd never thought there might be an actual family connection! And from the look on Mum's face, she hadn't either. She started to say something but was interrupted by Mr Tatters giving his beaky nose a good blow.

'Whilst we mourn his loss,' the lawyer repeated, dabbing his eyes, 'I am very pleased to tell you that your great-uncle remembered you in his will.' He picked up a leather-bound folder. Archie and Mum looked nervously at each other. Nobody had ever left them anything in a will before. They'd never known anyone with any money! All they knew was that Mr Tatters had sent them a letter asking them to drive all the way to the little town of Dundoodle, tucked between a mountain and a forest-edged loch, to meet him at Honeystone Hall to talk about some 'family business'. The lawyer was reading from a piece of paper in the folder.

'Your great-uncle writes: *As my nephew is no longer alive, I hereby leave all my earthly possessions to his son, my namesake, Archie McBudge. My fortune, my business holdings and associated properties I leave to him and his heirs.'* Mr Tatters took off his spectacles and looked at Archie expectantly.

'Oh, Archie!' said Mum with a deep intake of breath.

'What?' said Archie. He didn't understand. What were 'earthly possessions'? 'Has he left me his gardening tools or something?'

'No!' hissed Mum. 'Archie, he's left you *everything.'*

'Everything?' said Archie.

'*Everything,'* said Mr Tatters.

'Does that mean I *own* the fudge factory?' said Archie in disbelief. 'Where they make the fudge and the chocolates and all the other sweets?'

'Yes, Archie. You own the fudge factory,' confirmed Mr Tatters.

'And all the McBudge Fudge shops?' put in Mum, wide-eyed. 'There's one in almost every town.'

'And all the McBudge Fudge shops,' said Mr Tatters.

'And Honeystone Hall?' said Archie, looking around him. 'Can we come and live here? There must be over a hundred rooms in this place!' And a very odd painting, though he didn't mention that.

'*And* Honeystone Hall,' said Mr Tatters. He snapped the folder shut. 'Fudge fortune. Fudge factory. Fudge shops. Fudge … urm, *Honey*stone Hall. The whole lot. Even the gardening tools.'

I must have put my lucky underpants on today, thought Archie. He looked up at the portrait of Great-Uncle Archibald. The old man in the painting winked at him again. And this time, Archie winked back.

2

'There's one more thing,' said Mr Tatters, reaching into his jacket pocket. 'Your great-uncle left you this letter.' He handed Archie a crumpled envelope. A surprisingly steady hand (Great-Uncle Archibald looked *ancient* in the portrait) had written on it in thick caramel-brown ink:

To the heir of the Chief of the Clan McBudge.

'The heir,' said Mr Tatters, catching Archie's puzzled look. 'That would be you. Old Mr McBudge intended for you to read this in private. Why don't you go and explore whilst your mother and I discuss the legal paperwork and whatnot? I'm sure you'll find plenty of quiet spots in the house to read.'

He was being dismissed. The grown-ups had grown-up things to talk about. With a nod from Mum, Archie ran out of the library, clutching the mysterious letter. His head was spinning. He was … he was *rich*! And Honeystone Hall belonged to *him*. Him and nobody else. Except maybe the ghost of his great-uncle. What had been going on with that painting? He pushed it out of his mind. There were plenty of other things to think about. Great Things. It would take him a week just to explore the house, never mind the gardens and the factory.

Archie wandered along a passageway, pondering which of the doors to try first. Everything – furniture, pictures, wallpaper – looked *very* old and was covered in a ghostly layer of dust. The stillness was deathly. *Plenty of quiet spots*, Mr Tatters had said. Spots? This was practically measles.

He tried one door. It was a cupboard, filled with moth-speckled coats. Another door revealed an old-fashioned laundry room, with sinks and mangles and drying rails. So far, so disappointing. Yet there was something else. In each room Archie could feel a presence, like someone – some*thing* – had left just moments before. He shivered.

Finally, he chose a large green door with a dark metal handle. With a satisfying clunk, it opened and light poured into the shadowy passage. He took a step backwards as he was struck by the heat and smell of earth. Ferns, palm trees, vines and orchids lay before him, bathed in a balmy mist and occupied with the business of growing and flowering and generally being alive and leafy. Had he stumbled into a different world? Transported to a desert island? He half expected a dinosaur to lumber into view.

'It's a giant greenhouse,' he said aloud. The glass roof was as high as the Hall itself. The warmth, light and life were a marked contrast to the rest of the house and the dreary wintry world outside it. But it had the same watchfulness about it. Something hidden had its eye on him.

Archie followed a path amongst the plants and perched on a twisted tree root that had pushed its way up through the tiled floor. He opened the envelope and pulled out a crisp piece of paper covered with the same caramel-coloured writing.

Dear Archie (the letter began),

Mr Tatters must have told you by now that you are my heir as Chief of the Clan McBudge, as well as heir to the McBudge Fudge fortune. I have no doubt this will have come as a surprise to you. Knowing you would inherit one

day, but wanting you to have a normal life for as long as possible, your father kept his family connections a secret.

So Dad knew all along! Archie smiled. Dad loved secrets. He wished Dad was here now.

Your father was a clever man. Having lots of money can do strange things to people. And the desire for money can make people go bad. Very bad. You must always remember this!

But who better to run a chocolate factory than a child? Children understand fudge and sweets and chocolate far better than grown-ups. However, it is a great responsibility.

You must prove you are worthy of your inheritance, worthy of the name McBudge! So I have set you a test, in the form of a treasure hunt, to see just how canny you are …

There are six items you must collect, and six clues to find them. Once you have them all, a greater seventh treasure awaits you! But keep it secret! Others will go to any length to get it first!

Others? What did that mean?

The first clue will appear very soon. Keep your eyes open and your taste buds ready! You may find help in the strangest ways. Dundoodle is an odd place – expect the unexpected ...

Good luck!
Your great-uncle, Archibald McBudge.

Archie realised he was holding his breath. His heart was beating fast. A test? A treasure hunt?

P.S. Look behind you.

'If you ask me,' said a voice just by his ear, 'you're in a whole lot of trouble, Archie McBudge.'

3

Archie jumped up from his perch and spun round. There was a girl, hanging upside down from a thick vine that clung to the wall. Her grubby face glistened in the heat and gave him a cheeky upside-down smile. A spanner twirled confidently between her fingers.

'Who are you?' said Archie, annoyed. The girl unhooked her feet from the vine and let herself gently down to the ground.

'I'm Felicity Fairbairn,' said the girl, still smiling. 'Fliss for short.'

'I'm the McBudge heir,' said Archie. 'I own this place.' He liked the sound of that. But Fliss did not seem to be impressed.

'I know,' she said. 'I read your letter. What do you think the treasure is?'

'It's very rude to read over people's shoulders!' snapped Archie. So much for keeping things secret.

'It's also very *difficult* when you're topsy-turvy,' said Fliss. 'Anyway, it's your fault for sitting right underneath where I was working.' She pointed up to a moss-covered pipe threaded through the vine. 'There was a leaky pipe. I was fixing it, otherwise all old Mr McBudge's tropical plants – sorry, all *your* tropical plants, Mr McBudge *heir* – wouldn't have been heated properly and would die. There's no need to *thank* me or anything.'

'Thank you,' said Archie through gritted teeth. 'What did you mean when you said I was in trouble?'

'You'll never pass this test, this treasure-hunt-task-quest-thing or whatever it is,' said Fliss scornfully. 'You don't deserve to! How is it right that you get to have all *this* –' she waved her spanner around at the plants, the greenhouse and the Hall – 'when you don't know anything about this place? I've lived in Dundoodle my *whole* life, and my family have always worked in the McBudge factory. I know it like the back of my hand. But you're just a stranger here and don't even care about any of that. You've just turned up out of the blue and now it's all yours. It's *not fair*.'

She folded her arms emphatically and gave a sniff. Archie didn't have an answer. It wasn't fair really.

'I can't help it,' he said finally. 'Great-Uncle Archibald left it all to me. He didn't have to, I suppose. He could have left it to a home for bald, toothless donkeys called Clive if he'd wanted to. It's probably complicated.'

'That's why I like machines,' said Fliss, slapping the spanner into her palm. 'I'm going to be an engineer when I'm older. I know all about the machines in the factory. They're nice and simple. If they're broken, you can fix them. Or just smash them with a hammer.'

'And I'm going to fix this,' said Archie. 'I want to pass this test – and I will! I'll prove I'm a proper McBudge and show everyone that I *do* care.' For some reason the idea of Great Things had grown on him. What was Archie McBudge really capable of?

Fliss's frown softened.

'You sounded a bit like your great-uncle then,' she said, rubbing her dirty nose on her sleeve. 'Completely bonkers. You're *so* obviously going to need my help. Where shall we start?'

Archie sighed. This girl was not going to leave him alone.

'Can I trust you to keep this a secret?' he said.

'Of course!' said Fliss. 'But you should probably eat that letter if you want to be really sure.'

'What?' said Archie, looking at the wrinkled paper.

'Old Mr McBudge used to write on rice paper with chocolate ink. You can eat it! You could eat all his letters. I told you, *bonkers*.'

Archie sniffed the paper. It did smell good. He cautiously went to take a bite. The letter scrunched up in recoil and flew out of his hand and on to the floor.

'D-did you see that?' he said. 'The letter's *alive*!'

4

'*Expect the unexpected*,' said Fliss, wide-eyed. 'That was certainly unexpected.' She reached to touch the piece of paper. It jumped off the floor, jerkily flapping its folds like wings and rising into the air. They watched with open mouths as the letter flew once around Archie's head then up into a tree covered in purple, bell-shaped flowers, coming to rest on a branch.

At that moment a little white dog burst through the foliage, circling the tree and barking excitedly at the letter, which hopped and fluttered nervously like a bird.

'Sherbet!' a voice called from amongst the plants. 'Where are you? Heel, boy!' The dog completely ignored the command and ran up to Archie, wagging his tail. Then a very small and very, *very* old man appeared. He wheezed and coughed, leaning on the tree for support.

'Are you all right?' said Archie, forgetting the letter in the commotion.

'Oh, I'm just a tad out of breath,' croaked the man. 'You must be young Master Archie.' He stood straight and performed a wobbling bow. 'I'm Tablet, your butler. And you seem to have met Sherbet, your late great-uncle's dog. He recognises a McBudge, as do I. But I'm afraid I'm not up to walkies these days.'

Tablet looked like he had stepped out from inside a vacuum cleaner: grey dust knitted together with bits of hair and nail clippings. Every time he moved, flakes of skin gently drifted to the ground. He let out a scratchy cough to clear his throat and Archie half expected him to disintegrate on the spot.

'It's nice to meet you,' said Archie, cuddling the dog. A butler! Whatever next?

'I had the pleasure of serving your great-uncle,' Tablet said, his smile revealing a mixed selection of teeth. 'And his father too. I'm practically part of the furniture, you might say.' He gave a little laugh that turned quickly into a hacking cough, sending more bits of skin floating away in small clouds. *If he isn't part of the furniture, he's certainly all over it,* thought Archie, remembering the dust that covered everything in the library.

'I see you've fixed that pipe like I asked, Miss Fairbairn,' said Tablet, recovering himself. 'I'm much obliged. It's so nice to have some young people around the place. Or any *living* people, for that matter. I hope you'll be very happy here, Master Archie. I shall make sure I have the best room ready for you.'

'Completely bonkers,' hissed Fliss, as Tablet wobbled his way out of the greenhouse. 'He must be at least six-hundred years old.'

'I wonder if he knows about the treasure hunt,' said Archie, remembering the letter. It still sat on the tree branch.

And it wasn't alone.

5

'There are some birds up in the tree!' he said, releasing Sherbet. 'I'm sure they weren't there a moment ago.' Light filtering through the leaves played about their gleaming, jewel-coloured bodies.

'They're not birds,' said Fliss. 'Not exactly.' She clambered up the tree before Archie could say anything and plucked the seven colourful objects from the branch, chucking them down to him casually. The letter carefully kept out of her reach.

'Watch out!' said Archie. He anxiously juggled each bird as it fell. 'They look like glass!'

'No, they're not! They're McBudge Tweety Sweeties. You should know this – they're made in *your* factory! How did they get up here?'

Archie saw that the birds were made of boiled sugar, each one a different bright colour. They were hollow, with a hole in the tail and another in the beak.

'You blow through them and they sound a note,' said Fliss. 'The bigger the bird, the lower the note.' She picked a small blue bird and blew into the tail, forcing a husky whistle from the beak. Sherbet barked at the shrill noise. Archie tried a larger red bird, making a deeper sound.

'I think this is the first clue,' he said. 'The letter said to *Keep your eyes open and your taste buds ready*. Maybe all the clues are sweets.'

'But what does the clue *mean?*' said Fliss. 'Do you have to play a tune?'

Archie didn't know anything about music. He lined up the Tweety Sweeties in a row on the tree root, putting them in order of size. He crouched on the ground and blew through each one in turn, going from largest to smallest, then smallest to largest. Nothing happened.

'I don't think you'll ever be on *Dundoodle's Got Talent*,' said Fliss unhelpfully.

Archie frowned and studied the bird sweets. They had to be missing something. He noticed two of the birds had stuck together in the moist air. There was a kind of tab sticking out of one side of the first bird that had stuck in a hollow or slot on the side of the second bird next to it. All of the birds had a tab and a slot. They could all fit together, like a chain! Archie joined each bird to its neighbour, forming them into a fan shape with all the tail mouthpieces pointing the same way.

'You can blow through all of them at the *same time* – genius!' said Fliss gleefully. 'And completely bonkers.'

Archie put the joined-up tails into his mouth and blew. A soft harmony flowed from the birds, snaking through the tree, and sliding amongst the purple flowers. The tree quivered gently, nudging a single closed flower from its stalk. It tumbled to the ground in front of them and opened with a silvery chime, the petals curling back to reveal a small metal bell hidden inside. It bounced out of the flower, rolled across the tiles, and stopped at Archie's feet.

Archie and Fliss looked at each other.

'We are dealing with some *serious* magic here,' said Fliss. 'You're going to need all the help you can get.'

Mum appeared from behind a tree fern.

'There you are!' she said. 'And making friends already. That's good!'

Fliss smiled innocently. Archie quickly scooped up the bell and stuffed it into his pocket.

'We've got a dog!' he said, pointing to Sherbet, who wagged his tail politely.

Mum raised an eyebrow. 'Mr Tatters told me about some of the furry, four-footed details of the bequest,' she said. 'He'll have to come with us now. It's time to go home and sort out our move here, Archie. There's lots to do!'

Archie turned to say goodbye to Fliss.

'We can look for the next clue as soon as I'm back,' he whispered. She nodded and grinned, touching her spanner against her nose. Archie glanced up at the tree as he followed his mum out of the greenhouse. The magical letter had vanished.

6

It wasn't difficult to leave behind the grey, little house in the grey, rainy city of Invertinkle to move to Honeystone Hall in Dundoodle. Archie's home had lost its cheeriness after Dad died. And now he and his mum had all the money and comfort they could ask for. And a fresh start.

At first, Mum had been angry that Dad had never mentioned his rich relatives. She didn't like secrets, especially about money. But they had been happy in their modest way, and when Archie mentioned that, according to the letter, Dad had meant to protect them, she had smiled softly to herself in recognition.

'Your dad loved the countryside,' she sighed, as they drove through the forested valley on moving day. 'He would have liked us to live here.'

The road left the trees and followed the shore of the loch, the water's smooth surface glimmering like a mirror under the wintry sky. Dundoodle nestled amongst some low hills in the distance, overshadowed by the bad-tempered-looking mountain of Ben Doodle. Archie knew what the mountain was called as he had studied the town on a map. There was lots of countryside around Dundoodle, mostly moorland and forest. There would be plenty of exploring to do. Sherbet pressed his nose against the car window. He would certainly be glad to get back to his old stomping grounds!

'We mustn't go mad with the money,' continued Mum. 'We're not used to having it. It would be very easy to get carried away and spend it on silly things.'

'Yes, Mum,' said Archie.

'And you mustn't go mad with all the fudge and chocolate lying around,' said Mum. 'Or your teeth will be rotten in no time.'

'Yes, Mum,' said Archie.

'And you'll be all right in your new school, won't you?' said Mum. She was in full-on worrying mode.

'Yes, Mum!' said Archie. He hadn't really thought about the new school, the money (although that was nice) and the free fudge and chocolate (although that was nice too).

He'd been thinking about the Quest, as he had decided to call it, and what new magical clues and puzzles awaited him on their return. He had tucked the little bell safely into a wooden box that had belonged to his dad, hidden amongst his clothes in a suitcase. What could it be for?

The car wound through the twisty streets of Dundoodle. Archie hadn't paid much attention to the town on their first visit. But since the strange business with the letter and the Tweety Sweeties he noticed the whole place had an odd feel to it, just as the letter had said. The buildings were mostly old and crooked. There wasn't a single straight line to be seen amongst the beams and guttering and the rickety roof slates. It looked like the winter wind was trying to blow the whole town further up the slope of Ben Doodle and the houses were twisting around as they tried to stagger back down. All the people who lived there had the same odd, rickety look to them as well, as if they might easily have an elf or a wizard as a cousin, or a goblin as an auntie. *Or a ghost as a great-uncle*, thought Archie. What did old Mr McBudge have in store for him next?

Eventually they reached the McBudge factory. As their car passed the entrance, Archie watched the factory workers going about their business. The familiar McBUDGE sign was fixed over the tall iron gates, a

shield with a castle tower boldly painted on to it. Fierce little stone animals decorated the roofline of the factory. Honeystone Hall was right next door to the factory. Mr Tatters had told them there was a passageway that connected the two buildings.

'I wonder why it's called *Honey*stone Hall,' observed Mum as they turned into the driveway. 'Every building in this town is grey. Porridge-stone Hall would be a better name.'

'And there are statues of rats with wings everywhere,' said Archie. He spotted more of the little creatures adorning the Hall's roof.

'They're *dragons*. I think they're a family symbol or something,' said Mum absently, as she parked the car.

Archie saw that one dragon looked a little out of place, scrawnier and hunched. Suddenly, it jumped from the roof and flapped around the eaves, its beady little eyes glaring at him before it flew towards the town. Archie stifled a gasp. It wasn't a dragon, stone or otherwise, but some horrible-looking, bat-like thing. Had it been spying on them? Thankfully, Mum didn't seem to have noticed. She had enough to worry about already. But Archie shivered. How much more of Dundoodle's strangeness was he going to uncover?

7

They found the front door open. Sherbet immediately scurried into the hallway, glad to be back home, where Mr Tatters was waiting for them.

'Tablet will take care of your suitcases,' the lawyer said, as the old butler appeared from somewhere and wheezily heaved the car boot open. 'I need you to sign a few last bits of paper.' He led them back into the library. Archie gave the portrait of his great-uncle a hard stare but there were no blinks, winks or secret smiles today.

Mr Tatters had just handed over the keys to the Hall when they heard a furore outside. One shrill, insistent voice was raised over the others.

'Where *is* he? Where is that grubby little law-spouting, parrot-faced nonentity?' The library doors burst open and a thin, expensively dressed woman, a black handbag swinging from the crook of her arm, strode into the room. She was quickly followed by a short, sweating man and two well fed children that Archie thought he knew from somewhere. Tablet padded behind helplessly.

'So sorry, Master Archie!' said the butler. 'I couldn't stop them!'

'Titters!' spat the woman, advancing on the trembling lawyer. 'Wait till I get my hands on you!' Ten sharp, blood-red fingernails reached out for Mr Tatters, who hid behind his leather folder.

'Mrs Puddingham-Pye, please!' he begged. 'There is nothing more to be said. Old Mr McBudge's will was quite clear!'

'Cousin Jacqui?' said Mum, who seemed to recognise the woman. 'Is that *you*? You came to our wedding.'

The woman spun round on her heels, as if only seeing Archie and his mum for the first time.

'What?' she said, confused for moment.

'This is Dad's cousin, Jacqui,' said Mum to Archie. 'And her husband, Tosh Puddingham-Pye, and you two must be the twins, Georgie and Portia.' The short man gave a weak, sweaty smile. The twins just grunted like a pair of grumpy piglets and stared meanly at Archie. Cousin Jacqui did not looked pleased to see him either.

'It's an outrage!' she bellowed. 'Why would Great-Uncle Archibald, who I loved so, *so* deeply,' she clutched her claws to where Archie supposed her heart ought to be, 'and who I know *adored* me, leave everything to this ... this little *scrap* of a child, and not even a single penny to my loveable, *wuvable* little ones?'

Because he knew a greedy, grasping villain when he saw one! thought Archie. He remembered what the letter had said about how the desire for money could turn people bad.

'I'm *not* a scrap,' he said, quietly but firmly.

'And you're already a lady of considerable wealth, Mrs Puddingham-Pye,' soothed Mr Tatters. 'The

Puddingham-Pye Cookie Company is renowned. There's nothing better than a cup of tea with a P-P, as I always say.'

Archie sniggered. Mrs Puddingham-Pye glared at him.

'It was the secret ingredient of the fudge we wanted!' she growled. 'You've no doubt heard of our Yummo Cookie Finger Nibbles?'

Archie *had* heard of them. They were sold in boxes with a picture of two smirking children on it. That's where he had seen Georgie and Portia before!

'We were going to launch a whole new range of Yummo *Fudge* Cookie Finger Nibbles with the McBudge Fudge recipe, weren't we, pumpkin?' said Tosh Puddingham-Pye anxiously. He looked like a forlorn slug. Mrs Puddingham-Pye was definitely the one in charge.

'They would have been the jewel in the crown of the Puddingham-Pye Cookie Company,' said Jacqui. 'But Great-Uncle Archibald always refused to tell us what makes McBudge Fudge so irresistibly tasty – the secret ingredient!' She shook her fist at the portrait. 'And now we'll never have it!'

Archie caught the painting frowning at her. Mr Tatters coughed meekly.

'But now *you're* the McBudge heir, Mrs Puddingham-Pye,' he said.

'What?' said Mrs Puddingham-Pye, grasping him by his lapels. 'What's that, Totters? Speak up!'

'That is, erm … you see,' spluttered the lawyer, suddenly realising the awkwardness of the situation. 'If something *unfortunate* should befall Archie then you are next in line to inherit.'

It was the first time they had seen Mrs Puddingham-Pye smile. She released the lawyer and turned to look at Archie, bending her skinny frame in half until she was face-to-face with him.

'Then let's hope nothing *unfortunate* ever happens to darling little Urchin,' she said, all syrupy sweetness. She gave him a look like she could happily strangle him on the spot herself. Georgie and Portia giggled.

'My name is *Archie*,' said Archie defiantly, 'and I'll make my own fudge cookie fingers using *my* secret ingredient.'

Mrs Puddingham-Pye snarled. 'We'll see about that!' she said, her handbag swinging menacingly on her arm. 'Come along, Tosh – I'm not staying here a moment longer!' And with that, she sailed out of the room, her husband and children trailing in her wake. The library doors slammed shut behind the Puddingham-Pyes, making everyone jump.

'Goodness!' said Mum. 'It's as if the house itself were glad to be rid of them.'

If only Mum knew, thought Archie, smiling to himself.

8

'What do you want to do first?' said Mum as they stood in the hallway after having eventually seen Mr Tatters out. The apologetic lawyer had needed two cups of tea – with four sugars in each – *and* a P-P to recover from the attentions of Mrs Puddingham-Pye. 'Explore the house? Or look around the town?'

'I'd like to see the factory,' said Archie. He wanted to look for clues for the Quest but thought he ought to see the McBudge business first. He hadn't forgotten Fliss's angry outburst, and wanted to show he was taking his inheritance seriously.

'That's what I like to hear!' said a cheery voice from the doorway. They turned to see a smiling man wearing a white coat with a *McBUDGE* badge on the front. He had a red nose and kept sniffing like he had a bad cold. 'Scotty Hankiecrust, factory manager, reporting for duty, Mr McBudge! Glad to see you're as keen as old Mr McBudge was. Allow me to give you a personal tour.'

'I hope there will be plenty of chocolate and fudge samples to eat ... um, inspect,' said Archie, trying to sound like a factory owner.

'Oh yes, Mr McBudge,' grinned Mr Hankiecrust. 'Of course, sir.'

Archie, Mum and Sherbet followed the sniffing Mr Hankiecrust down the passageway that led from the house to the factory. As soon as they opened the factory door they were surrounded by the noise of machinery: stirring, chopping, mixing, baking and packing. The factory was huge and buzzed with activity. Sweets, chocolates and fudge hurtled past them on conveyor belts, on their way to being tasted, sorted and boxed up for sale. The factory manager showed Archie and his mum the enormous vats filled with sugary liquids and melted chocolate ready to be turned into tasty treats; how the chocolate was piped and swirled over centres of coloured sugar or whipped, foaming fondant; and how the fudge was simmered in giant pans until just the right temperature, before cooling into slabs of soft, golden delight. Archie tasted as many sweets as

possible – for business reasons, of course.

'In our research laboratory, I can let you see our latest designs for new products,' said Mr Hankiecrust excitedly. He ushered them through a door into a room where lots of people in white coats were standing around with clip-boards and looking very earnestly at different sweets. Sherbet sniffed the air and drooled.

'This is our newest brainwave,' said Mr Hankiecrust. He pointed at what looked like an ordinary piece of chocolate. 'A Chewochocochunk. It's a type of fudge chewing gum, covered in chocolate.' Archie picked up the Chewochocochunk and popped it into his mouth.

'What do you think, sir?' enquired Mr Hankiecrust. The people in white coats all held their breath.

'*Mmfgggbberrchoooeey*,' was all Archie could manage to say.

'Yes,' laughed Mr Hankiecrust. 'It is a bit too chewy perhaps. We'll have to work on that one.' The people in white coats all scribbled on their clipboards busily.

After they had left the laboratory, the factory manager took them to his office.

'I just wanted a quiet word,' he said as they sat around his desk. He looked anxiously at Archie and his mum and spoke in a whisper, even though there was no one else about. 'We have a bit of a problem. No one has been able to find the secret ingredient for the famous McBudge Fudge since your great-uncle died.'

'Isn't that what the Puddingham-Pyes were after?' said Archie, who was still picking Chewochocochunk out of his teeth.

'Oh, you've met them, have you?' snorted Mr Hankiecrust. 'Yes, they'd love to get their hands on it. But the fact is, no one knows what it is or where it's kept. Old Mr McBudge didn't tell anybody.' He produced a plate with two piles of identical-looking fudge. Archie and his mum each took a chunk of fudge from the first pile. It was nice but very ordinary.

'Now try the McBudge Fudge,' said Mr Hankiecrust, pointing to the other pile. Archie stuffed a generous piece of fudge into his mouth. It was creamier, sweeter and richer than the first, soft and delicious. As soon as he swallowed it he wanted another piece.

'*Mmmmmm*,' he and Mum said together.

'We've got a stockpile of McBudge Fudge we can send out to the shops,' said Mr Hankiecrust, 'but if we don't find the secret ingredient soon any new batches of fudge we make just won't be the same. It'll just be *ordinary* fudge.'

'Does that matter?' said Mum. 'The factory makes loads of other things.'

'But fudge is our biggest seller by far,' said Mr Hankiecrust. 'If we don't find the secret ingredient soon, it could be a *disaster*!'

9

Mum and Archie looked at each other, shocked. There had been no talk of any secret ingredient in the will *or* in the letter Great-Uncle Archibald had left for Archie.

'It's probably mentioned somewhere amongst all the papers that Mr Tatters gave us,' suggested Mum.

'We'll do some investigating at the Hall,' promised Archie. 'It must be there.'

Mr Hankiecrust seemed a bit happier after that. Mum wanted to talk some more with him about how the factory worked, so Archie and Sherbet went off to explore on their own.

They climbed some steps up to a gangway that hung over the factory floor. It gave a great view of everything that was going on. They walked further along and

upwards, where the gangway was surrounded on all sides by large, twisting pipes like the tree trunks and vines of a metal jungle. Jets of steam spurted from valves and shrouded their path in a billowing mist. Odd gurgling and clanking noises echoed around them as they walked. To Archie's ears it sounded like something was being digested in the belly of a large beast nearby. It was all very eerie.

CRASH! A large sack landed heavily in front of him, missing him by centimetres and rattling the gangway so that he staggered backwards. The sack burst and Sherbet yelped in alarm. A white cloud of icing sugar erupted and enveloped them. Archie coughed as he breathed in the sweet powder. How had that happened? He looked up into the darkness and could just see two faces peeking over the side of another gangway, higher up in the roof. The faces disappeared with a giggle and a snort. The Puddingham-Piglet twins! Had they dropped the sack of sugar deliberately? He brushed the white dust off his clothes as he remembered Mrs Puddingham-Pye's veiled threat. He would have to watch out.

He had only walked on a few more steps when there was a whistle from behind the tangle of metalwork ahead.

'Who's there?' called Archie. The twins again? Sherbet gave a short bark and disappeared around a corner. Archie followed cautiously. The gangway was empty – the dog had vanished!

'Sherbet? Where are you?'

A hand reached out from behind a large pipe and grabbed his collar, dragging him into the shadows.

'Welcome back,' whispered a voice he recognised. It was Fliss! A light was switched on and Archie found himself on a platform wedged amongst the pipework and completely hidden from the gangway. It was almost like a cave, or a treehouse where the tree branches were all made of metal.

'I thought you were the Puddingham-Pyes!' said Archie with relief. 'I think they're trying to get rid of me.'

'You'll be safe here,' said Fliss. She grinned at him. 'This is my secret hideout. I can stay in the factory all day and no one knows where I am. It's been used by other children throughout the years but I'm the only person who uses it now.' There were tools lying about, some comics and books, and drawings of machines and aeroplanes. A couple of stools and a lamp stood in a corner whilst some drink cartons sat on a bookshelf, along with a selection of McBudge confectionery products that Archie suspected had probably been pinched from a nearby conveyor belt. Sherbet sniffed around suspiciously.

'You've timed your arrival perfectly,' said Fliss. 'We have an appointment.'

'With who?' said Archie.

'Someone who can help us with your treasure hunt thingie.'

'It's a *quest*. And it's a supposed to be a secret!

Why not tell the whole of Dundoodle whilst we're at it?'

'Pardon me for wanting to help you with your fancy-pants quest! I thought you might need some expert help. Quiet – I can hear him now.'

'An expert?' said Archie. 'Who is it?'

'Billy Macabre,' whispered Fliss, peering through the pipes. Archie looked though a gap and saw a small, scrawny boy with large haunted eyes walking along the gangway. He was dressed from head-to-toe in black, and carried a heavy-looking black bag which he clutched to his chest.

'*That's* our expert?' said Archie. The boy was younger than either of them.

'Yes!' snapped Fliss. 'His real name is Billy MacCrabbie but he says "Macabre" makes him sound more enigmatic.'

'More like *completely bonkers*,' said Archie. The boy appeared at the entrance to the hideout. He looked from Fliss to Archie and frowned.

'This is Archie,' said Fliss. 'He's the client I was telling you about, Billy.'

'Client?' said Archie.

'My card,' said Billy curtly, presenting Archie with a

small piece of paper. Written on it in scruffy handwriting
were the words:

> **William Q. Macabre, Esq.**
> **Paranormal Investigator**
> **Wyrdiness is My Business.**

10

'Archie and I need your help, Billy,' whispered Fliss. 'There have been *mysterious happenings*.'

'Mystery is my natural abode,' said Billy in a gruff monotone, as if he were advertising a horror film. 'I live in the shadows.'

'Your card says you live at 14 Bluebell Avenue,' said Archie, reading the back of the piece of paper. Billy gave him a superior look.

'That is my *base of operations*,' said Billy, dropping the horror voice. 'My investigations can take me to parts both perilous and supernatural.' He paused. 'As long as I'm back for tea, or my mum will kill me.'

'Billy is an expert on all the magical stuff in Dundoodle,' Fliss explained as they sat down on the floor of the hideout, with Sherbet curling up for a snooze in Archie's lap. She handed them both a McBudge Jelly Toad from her stash. 'Billy knows *everything*.'

'Is there lots of magical stuff?' said Archie, chewing the toad. It was a very odd-looking town with odd-looking people. He could well believe Honeystone Hall wasn't the only place with secrets.

'It's *wyrdiness*,' corrected Billy. He opened the bag and brought out several exercise books that were bound together with string. On the cover of the first book was the hand-written title:

The ~~Ensyklo~~ Book of Wyrdiness of Dundoodle
and its Surroundings
By William Q. ~~MacCrabbie~~ Macabre

The rest of the cover was decorated with tinfoil stars and magical symbols drawn in felt-tip pen. Billy opened the book to the first page, which had a photocopied drawing of a tree stuck on to it. The drawing looked like it had been taken from the kind of book found in a museum, as it was surrounded by words in an old-fashioned style of writing.

'This is the Wyrdie Tree,' said Billy, speaking in a slow, solemn voice. 'It's a tree that's supposed to grow in the middle of the forest by the loch. It's the oldest tree in the forest, if not the whole world. Its roots reach deep, deep underground, stretching for miles, even under Dundoodle itself.'

Archie remembered the tree root that had broken through the floor of the greenhouse.

'What's so special about this tree?' he said.

'The roots go so deep they touch the magic locked in the earth, the leftover magic from when the world formed. The tree draws the magic up into its roots and inside itself. Wherever the Wyrdie Tree's roots spread, they spread the magic with them. It makes Dundoodle a hot spot for strange creatures and unusual occurrences.'

'Billy collects all the stories about Dundoodle,' said Fliss with admiration, 'and puts them in his book. His knowledge could help us. This isn't an ordinary quest. It's a *magical* one.'

'I am Dundoodle's foremost expert on all the old

legends about the small folk, gnomes and magical people.' said Billy. 'Wobble-gobbles, wyrdie-birds and wigzits are a speciality. I also have a sideline in investigating ghostly hauntings, and know everything there is to know about graveyards. For instance, would you care to speculate on how many different types of maggots feed on dead bodies?'

'Two?' Archie guessed, wrinkling his nose.

'*Twelve*,' said Billy. 'My schoolteacher says I have an "unnatural interest",' he added proudly.

'Have you actually seen any of these wyrdie-whatsits or whatever they are?' said Archie. Billy looked uncomfortable for a moment.

'Not *exactly*,' he said. 'But everyone knows Dundoodle is odd.'

'*Everyone*,' agreed Fliss. 'You must have felt it. My granny said she'd seen the tree sprites of Dundoodle forest when she was little. They're meant to be a bit stupid because their heads are full of woodworm. And Mr Tavish from the supermarket says he's heard the cry of the Beast of Glen Bogie, the legendary and really, really annoyed giant vole. Then there is the Waggott family. They're supposed to be descended from local were-badgers.'

'There's a Waggott at our school,' said Billy, 'who's already shaving.'

'Poor Fiona,' said Fliss. 'She's only six.'

'And let's not forget Pookiecrag Castle, of course,' said Billy.

'Pookiecrag Castle?' said Archie, the hairs on the back of his neck tingling at the name. 'I saw that on a map. It's on an island at the other end of the loch.'

'You *should* know it,' said Fliss. 'It's the old McBudge ancestral home, so it probably belongs to you along with everything else around here. The McBudges had to move out and build Honeystone Hall to live in instead.'

'Why?' said Archie.

'Because,' said Fliss, lowering her voice to a whisper, 'it's the most *haunted* place in the whole of Dundoodle.'

11

'The *most* haunted?' said Archie with a shiver. This inheritance had turned out to be quite a mixed bag.

'Oh yes!' said Billy, in his element. 'Eerie flickering shapes fly amongst the shadows of its ruins on many a dark night, and the sounds of hell-spawn digging their way through the earth emanate from its dungeons.'

'But Honeystone Hall seems to have its fair share of wyrdiness too,' said Archie. He described the strange creature he had seen on the roof earlier.

'That sounds like a mobgoblin!' said Billy, excitedly flicking through the pages of his book. 'I can't believe you've actually seen one! It's got a rating of six out of ten on the Macabre Creepy Scale.' He took a pen out of his bag and scribbled some notes on to a page that had the heading *Mobgoblins, Harpydarps & Other Wyrdie-Birds*. 'Some gargoyles you see on old buildings are meant to be mobgoblins that have been turned to stone. They were used as messengers and spies by witches and wizards.' Archie frowned. So the creature *had* been watching him and his mum. But spying for *who*?

'What do you know about flying letters, Billy?' said Fliss slowly, as Sherbet began to growl.

'Never heard of such a thing,' said Billy emphatically. 'Are you sure … ?' he began, but stopped as a piece of folded paper flapped past his nose and came to a rest on top of his head. 'I-I'd give that a rating of five out of ten on the Macabre Creepy Scale,' said Billy with a gulp.

'It's my letter!' said Archie. 'It's back!' Sherbet leaped from his lap, knocked Billy flat and chased the fluttering object out of the hideout. The children ran after the excitable dog, who stalked the flying paper as it skipped and hopped along the gangway. It led them down some stairs and through a set of swing doors.

'This is the packing area,' said Fliss, 'where they box up all the sweets for delivery.' Piles of boxes of all sizes were stacked around the room. Everyone working was far too busy to give three children and a dog a second look, and certainly didn't see the letter sailing silently over their heads. It slipped through a doorway at one side of the room which had *Seconds and Damaged Goods* written on a sign next to it. Archie and the others crept through the door and found themselves surrounded by more boxes, but some of these were dented and torn.

'If anyone drops or breaks anything it ends up here,' said Fliss, 'until they work out what to do with it.'

The letter had settled on the top of the tallest pile of boxes and didn't move. It was much too high to reach and the boxes looked far too wobbly to climb. Sherbet sat and stared at it. He was not going to let it out of his sight again.

'The letter's brought us here for a reason,' said Archie. 'Remember how it showed us where the first clue was, by flying into the tree? I think the next task of the Quest is in this room.'

'I think so too,' said Fliss, picking up a smaller box that was sat on its own. 'Look!'

Unlike all the other packaging, with their colourful labels, the box was plain and undecorated. On its top, written in distinctive caramel-brown ink, was the word ARCHIE. Archie carefully lifted the lid and held his breath, nervous of what might be inside. It was filled with small pieces of a shiny treacle-coloured substance. Archie recognised it at once.

'It's toffee,' he said. 'Lots and lots of little bits of toffee.'

'That's a bit disappointing,' said Billy, peering over Archie's shoulder. 'I was expecting a mystical shrunken head or at least a blood-covered dagger.'

Fliss screwed up her nose. 'In a chocolate factory?' she said. 'All the clues are going to be sweets. I think we can be certain of that now.'

'Then it's a shame it's broken,' said Billy. 'A dead end before we've even begun.'

'Wait a second – maybe it's meant to be broken!' said Archie. 'Look, it's like a jigsaw puzzle.' He showed them one of the larger pieces. 'There's a picture in the toffee. I can't tell what it is, but if we fit these bits together it might show us something.'

He gently tipped out the pieces on to the floor and sighed. There were hundreds of them! It was going to take ages.

'This isn't the best use of my talents,' said Billy with a sniff. 'Let me know when you're done and actually have something mystical for me to look at.'

Fliss grabbed the boy by the sleeve as he edged towards the door.

'Three heads are better than one,' she said firmly. 'If we work together we can get this solved quickly!'

Archie smiled at her gratefully as Billy grudgingly knelt next to him. The three children bent over the toffee jigsaw and got to work. They were soon engrossed in fitting all the little pieces together.

So engrossed that they were unaware someone was *watching* them …

12

'We're almost there!' said Archie. They had been kneeling on the floor of the *Seconds and Damaged Goods* room for ages. The toffee jigsaw puzzle was practically finished. There was just one corner left to do.

'Thank goodness,' said Billy, chewing on a damaged piece of McBudge Strawberry String that he had 'rescued'. 'I can't believe I've spent so much time *looking* at toffee rather than eating it.'

'But what is the picture meant to be?' said Fliss. They studied the cracked oblong shape they had created. There were lines and squares somehow drawn through the toffee, giving it the look of a stained glass window.

'I think it's a plan of a building,' said Archie. 'Showing

all the different rooms and how they connect to each other.'

'Is it the factory?' said Fliss. 'Honeystone Hall?' Archie shrugged.

'Wait – we've still got to finish this corner of the puzzle,' he said. They hurriedly sorted the final pieces into place, an extra bit of the picture emerging from the remaining bits of toffee.

'What is it?' said Fliss. 'Is it a bat?'

'Or a mobgoblin?' said Billy.

'No,' said Archie. 'It's a little dragon. Look – it's pointing its claw at one of the rooms in the plan.'

'What for?' said Billy.

'Perhaps it's pointing to the location of the final treasure,' said Archie. The others' eyes lit up with excitement.

'It's a *treasure map*!' said Fliss.

'I'm sure I've seen this place somewhere,' said Billy, scratching his chin.

Before he could say anything more, there was a sniffing noise behind them and Mr Hankiecrust appeared in the doorway. It was too late to hide the toffee jigsaw.

'Hello, kids,' the factory manager grinned. 'I thought I heard you in here. The factory will be closing soon so

you'd better finish your game. I wouldn't want you to get trapped inside when the lights go out. Although at least you wouldn't go hungry!' He gave a chuckle and a sniff at the same time, which ended up as a kind of mucus-filled snort. The children smiled weakly.

'Do you think he saw the picture?' whispered Fliss after Mr Hankiecrust had left.

'It doesn't matter,' said Archie. 'He doesn't know about the Quest. He just thought we were playing.'

Meanwhile, Billy had opened his book and was drawing a copy of the jigsaw's picture into it.

'That way we can eat the toffee,' he said, licking his lips. 'We don't want to be carrying it around with us all the time.'

They gathered up the bits of the jigsaw and put them back in the box – 'It's too precious to eat,' said Archie, much to Billy's annoyance – along with Billy's sketch. Then they made their way back to Fliss's hideout. The letter had gone, disappearing when they were distracted by Mr Hankiecrust, but Archie wasn't surprised.

'I reckon the letter only shows up to lead us to the clues,' he said, as they stored the box in a nook amongst the pipes.

'It's a messenger from beyond the grave,' said Billy. 'Guided by your great-uncle's spirit, using undead ecto-plasmic wyrdie-forces.'

Fliss shivered.

'Let's just say it's *magic*, shall we?' she said. 'And leave the undead out of it. So that's two clues dealt with. I wonder what's next.'

It was getting late and the factory bell rang to signal it was about to close, so they agreed to meet up the next day at the Hall. Archie watched Fliss and Billy leave by the main factory doors, along with all the workers, before he and Sherbet ran down the connecting passageway to the house.

They found Mum in the library, sitting at his great-uncle's old wooden desk, and surrounded by papers.

'I've been looking for anything to do with this missing secret ingredient,' she said, looking tired, 'but no luck so far. What we will do if we can't find it? Mr Hankiecrust sounded very concerned.' Archie had completely forgotten about the McBudge Fudge secret ingredient! He ought to be taking more interest but he hadn't been able to stop thinking about the Quest. Responsibility was hard work.

'Don't worry, Mum,' he said. 'It'll turn up somewhere.' He stared at the painting of Great-Uncle Archibald, hoping for some sign, but none came.

Just then, Tablet appeared at the door with hot chocolate and toast covered in rhubarb jam. He may not have been good at dusting but he certainly seemed to know when some comforting food and drink were needed. Mum and Archie curled up with their tea on the comfy leather sofa by the fire, whilst Sherbet nestled between them, snuffling for the occasional dropped crust. Archie was bursting to tell Mum about everything that had happened but he could see she had plenty on her mind already. He licked melted butter and crumbs from his fingers. *I'll keep quiet for now*, he thought.

13

There was an icy feel to the breeze when Archie met Fliss and Billy at the front door of the Hall the next morning.

'Dad says that snow is on its way,' said Fliss, stepping into the hallway and heaving off her winter coat.

'If it is then you should be careful,' said Billy darkly. 'It's the favourite weather of the blue-bottomed pixies of Ben Doodle. Their full moon ritual is famously horrifying.'

Billy had never been inside the Hall before and was impressed by the majestic old building with its cobweb-filled nooks and crannies.

'It's a veritable nexus of arcane energies,' he declared. 'You can smell the wyrdiness in the air!'

'I think that's probably mothballs,' said Fliss. Archie

showed Billy the tree root in the greenhouse and he immediately started making notes and sketching in his book.

A sudden bark and a whine from Sherbet alerted them to the arrival of the magical letter, hovering overhead.

'Here we go again,' said Fliss. The letter flapped around a palm tree and then banked away into the depths of the greenhouse. Archie tore at the overgrown vines to clear a path as they followed. They spotted the letter resting on the handrail of a metal spiral staircase that was weighed down with moss and ivy. After a scramble to the top of the stairs, they found a door tucked behind a curtain of foliage. Archie pushed it open. In front of them a line of sweets led down a gloomy passageway. They were all different types and colours, scattered along the floor seemingly at random.

'I think we're meant to follow the trail,' said Archie. Leaving the letter perched by the door, they ran along the passage and tracked the sweets as they led up another set of stairs to the next floor. Sherbet scampered ahead, sniffing the moth-eaten carpet like a bloodhound.

'Hurry up, Billy!' called Fliss. He was some way behind, busily stuffing his pockets with sweets.

'My mum says it's a crime to waste good food,' came

the reply from a mouth filled with chocolate. 'And these are *really* good.' They entered another long corridor.

'I've not really explored the Hall yet,' said Archie, glancing in the doorways of a couple of the rooms as they passed. 'I wonder if I'll ever find out how big it is!'

'It doesn't look like anyone has been this way for years, apart from the resident spiders,' Fliss remarked. 'Or maybe this is where Tablet stores the spare dust.'

The trail ended in front of a door. Archie carefully pushed it open. The huge room behind it was empty of furniture, but there were three doors on the opposite wall. The floor of the room was covered in thousands of sweets. It was quite a sight.

'A veritable candy carpet!' said Billy, practically drooling. He put a foot forward, but Archie stopped him.

'There's a pattern made out of the sweets,' Archie

said. 'Look at how they are arranged in zigzagging lines.'

'A maze!' said Fliss, clapping her hands.

'Calm down!' said Billy. 'I'm amazed too.'

'No! It's a *maze*. Like you get in a puzzle book. The sweets make up the walls of the maze. You have to follow the right route and avoid the dead ends to get to the other side.'

It was easy enough to see where the maze started: there was only one entrance. But they could see there were three exits, each leading to one of the doors on the other side of the room. The path of the maze was just wide enough for someone to tiptoe through if they were careful. Archie went first, followed by Fliss, then Billy. Sherbet watched from the edge of the room, his head tilted to one side in confusion at the humans' strange behaviour.

Like tightrope walkers, they travelled along the maze in a wobbly line until the path divided in two.

'We should split up and go after both trails,' said Billy. 'That's what they would do on *Dougie McFly, Spectre Detector*. I've watched every episode.'

'You both carry on,' said Archie. 'I'll go down the other route.'

After a while, Billy and Fliss met another junction and each took a different way.

'Three paths and three doors,' said Archie. 'Which leads where?'

But they were in for a surprise. All three paths finished in dead ends.

'That doesn't make sense,' said Fliss, scratching her head. 'One path has to go somewhere.'

'Hang on a minute,' said Archie. He studied the sweets that blocked the trail. 'For each path the way is blocked by the same type of sweet. What are they? I've seen them before.'

'They're McBudge Traffic Light Chews,' said Billy. 'They come in three colours – red, orange and green.'

'Look – both of your trails have a red chew blocking them. Mine has a green chew.'

'So?' said Fliss and Billy together.

'They're Traffic Light Chews,' Archie reminded them. 'Green for go and red for stop. What if it's some kind of code? This is supposed to be a test, remember.'

'So if red means stop, then perhaps we're not supposed to follow those paths in the maze,' Fliss suggested.

'Exactly!' said Archie. 'This green chew isn't blocking

the way, it's telling me to carry on.' He stepped over the chew and continued along the sweet-lined path. Eventually Archie made it all the way to the other side of the maze, to the third door in the wall. Fliss, Billy and Sherbet joined him as he opened the door. Behind it was a narrow, winding staircase.

'We're in one of the towers,' guessed Archie, as they clambered upwards.

At the top of the stairs was another door. They were puffing and panting from the climb, with Billy in particular weighed down by a bag now crammed with sweets he'd collected along the way. It took all their efforts to push the door open, its long-unused hinges grinding with splintered rust. They entered a small, round, dark room, empty except for a table. It was very cold, the winter wind piercing the cracks in the crumbling stone wall. Billy rubbed the dirty glass of one of the three windows, letting in light that painted the cobwebs silver.

'We're quite high up,' he said, peering out. 'You can see right over the loch.'

'That's Pookiecrag Castle in the distance,' said Fliss, looking over his shoulder. Grey, ruined towers peeked over the tops of the dark forest which grew on the island at the far end of the lake. The tiny, fluttering shapes of crows circled the castle. It did look like the perfect location for a bit of haunting.

But Archie was more interested in what was on the table: a triangular wooden box. What could be inside it? There was no lid, but the surface was carved with three little dragons arranged around a star. There were three sweets in front of the box, little jelly animals of different colours – gold, green and white.

'Dragums!' said Billy. 'Gummy dragons. McBudge don't make many of those. They're very rare.' *Dragons again*, thought Archie. They seemed to be everywhere.

'Is it another colour-code puzzle?' said Fliss.

'I think so,' said Archie. 'But not traffic lights this time. The shape of the carvings and the shape of the sweets match. Maybe we place a Dragum on each dragon. But which one goes where?'

'We need to crack the code!' said Fliss. What could the colours mean? Archie and Fliss sat in silent thought whilst Billy paced the room, passing in front of the window he had cleaned earlier. Every time he passed it, he blocked the beam of sunlight, casting a Billy-shaped shadow over one corner of the box.

'Keep still, Billy!' scolded Fliss. 'We can't see the clues without the light.'

Archie smacked his fist into his hand.

'I think I've got it!' he said. 'The sunlight from that window points straight to one of the dragons. What I mean is, the *dragon* is pointing towards the *window*.'

Fliss and Billy gathered round the table.

'So?' said Fliss.

'Each of the dragons is pointing towards a different window. What if the colours relate to something we can see from each window?'

Billy and Fliss ran to the other windows, hastily clearing away the dirt with their sleeves.

'I can see Ben Doodle,' said Fliss. 'The top is covered with snow already.'

'And I can see the old forest,' said Billy. 'The Wyrdie Tree is in there somewhere.'

'I'll put the white Dragum on the dragon facing the white mountain,' said Archie, chewing his lip thoughtfully. 'The green Dragum on the dragon facing the green forest. That leaves the gold Dragum facing Pookiecrag Castle, though I'm not sure why.'

He positioned the sweets on the carvings. As soon as the gold Dragum was in place, there was a click from inside the box. The star at the centre opened as a little trapdoor drew back, and a golden egg emerged from inside, pushed up by some unseen clockwork mechanism.

'The golden dragon has given you a golden dragon's egg!' said Billy. 'Awesome!'

'A golden sugar egg,' said Archie, picking it up and giving it a sniff. He gently tapped it with a finger. The sugar crumbled in his hand, turning to glittering dust. A small metal object was all that remained.

'It's a ring.' He passed it to Fliss.

'It looks like gold,' she said, turning it over. 'And there's a picture on it – a shield with a castle tower. Isn't that on the McBudge Fudge labels?'

Before anyone could answer, there came a *CRASH!* and an '*OUCH!*' from the stairs. Someone was outside the door.

14

'Who left all these gob-bothering sweets lying around?' said a crotchety voice.

Sherbet yapped in recognition. The children peered out into the stairwell.

'Tablet!' said Archie. 'What are *you* doing here?' The old butler was lying in a heap on the steps, rubbing his bottom miserably. He had a feather duster in his other hand.

'Just doing a bit of dusting, Master Archie,' he explained. 'It's been a while since I've been up in the north tower. But I slipped on one of these sweets that seem to be everywhere – very dangerous, I must say.'

'Sorry,' said Billy guiltily. 'I think my bag has a hole in it.'

They helped the butler to his feet. There didn't seem to be any harm done, apart from a bruised backside. Tablet noticed the gold ring in Archie's hand.

'Why, Master Archie, you've found the Ring of the McBudges!' he said in surprise. 'It's been passed down from one chief of the Clan McBudge to the next for centuries. I've not seen it since your great-uncle died.'

'What's so special about it?' said Archie.

'Maybe it's cursed by an ancient dwarf ring-maker to crush your finger every time you pick your nose,' said Billy. 'Or possessed by an undead spirit that will freeze your finger until it goes blue and drops off.'

'Nonsense!' gurgled Tablet in amusement. 'Only a McBudge is allowed to wear it. It's proof that you're a member of the family.' He pointed towards the window. 'The tower on the shield represents Pookiecrag Castle.' The butler made his wobbling way back to the door. 'I'm sure you'll find out more about it in the library,' he said. 'There are lots of books on the family's history there.' He disappeared back down the stairs. There was a distant *CRASH!* followed by a number of thuds as he found some more of the gob-bothering sweets on his way.

'Was he keeping an eye on us?' said Fliss. 'It's funny how he happened to be in this part of the Hall at the same time. And he didn't even stay to do any dusting!'

'I don't believe that story about doing housework,' said Billy. 'Unless he was just *rearranging* the dust.'

Archie put the ring into his pocket.

'Maybe he was being helpful,' he said. 'Either way, it's one more puzzle solved. Three more to go!'

A shadow passed in front of one of the windows. They turned, hearing a dull scraping sound of leather wings against the glass pane.

'It's that *thing* again,' Archie cried, springing over to the window and forcing its ancient metal frame open. He winced as he felt a blast of cold against his face. 'The mobgoblin!'

Billy and Fliss crowded around his shoulders to watch the strange creature flapping about the tower. It scowled at them, its weaselly face full of nasty-looking teeth. Archie leaned dangerously out of the window to grab at it, but the little demon squawked angrily and lurched out of reach. It sped away, soon lost amongst the rickety rooftops of the neighbouring town.

'A mobgoblin – finally I've *seen* one!' said Billy in delight. 'I'm going to change my rating to at least six point five out of ten on the Macabre Creepy Scale.

Did you see its
yellow beady
eyes? Fantastic!'
He tugged his
book out of his bag
and began scribbling
furiously.

'We're not *bird-
watching*!' said Archie
in frustration. 'Some-
one is using that
thing to spy on us!
As if I didn't have
enough to worry
about.'

Billy looked
taken aback. Fliss
frowned.

'Who yanked your gold chain?' she scolded. 'What
exactly have *you* got to worry about, Moneybags
McBudge?'

Archie sighed.

'I'm sorry,' he said. From inheriting the factory
to the magical Quest, from the mysterious mobgoblin to

the villainous Puddingham-Pyes – he hadn't realised just how much it had all weighed down on him. And then there was the missing secret ingredient! He told Billy and Fliss all about it. 'I know there are people far worse off than me. And I am really glad you're helping me. But I've hardly stopped for breath since I arrived in Dundoodle yesterday.' Fliss smiled kindly.

'You've got *us* to help you!' she said. 'My brains, Billy's knowledge and Sherbet's nose. The P-Ps are just a bunch of bullies, all flashy wrapper but hollow inside, like a cheap Easter egg. And the secret ingredient will turn up somewhere, I'm sure of it.'

'It's probably in an old sock,' suggested Billy. 'That's where I seem to find things. I blame the Dundoodle dust-buggits, they're always moving things around. They've a one out of ten rating on the Macabre Creepy Scale.' Fliss gave Billy a you-are-not-helping look.

'As for the mobgoblin,' she said, 'if it *is* spying on us, then it'll be back' – there was a glint in her eye – 'and the next time it appears we'll be *ready* …'

15

They made their way back downstairs, Billy collecting
the trail of sweets in his bag ('For closer study later on,' he
said), and eventually they found a corridor that Archie
recognised as the one leading to his bedroom. There, he put
the Ring of the McBudges alongside the bell in his dad's
wooden box, that he had hidden at the back of his wardrobe. Sherbet decided it was time for a nap, yawning and
snuggling into the covers on Archie's bed. Billy yawned too.

'I didn't realise hunting for treasure could be so
exhausting,' he said. 'We must have walked miles up and
down all your stairs. And I seem to have a tummyache for
some reason.'

'Let's call it a day,' said Archie, grinning. 'Will you be
back tomorrow?'

'Tomorrow is Monday,' called Fliss. 'So we won't be able to come over until after school. Try and do something normal and non-magical in the meantime.'

Archie smiled gratefully. He wasn't due to start at the school until after the Christmas holidays, so he would have to get used to spending the days by himself. At least he had Sherbet for company, when the dog wasn't snoozing.

Archie showed the others out. He was halfway back up the stairs when he heard a car draw up outside. Thinking it was Mum returning from the shops, he ran down to open the door for her. His heart sank. Instead of their little beige car, there was a gleaming silver limousine with Mrs Puddingham-Pye at the wheel. Sitting on the back seat were Georgie and Portia. They grinned evilly at him.

'I met your mother out shopping, Urchin,' said Mrs Puddingham-Pye, her long, thin neck oozing out of the car window like a snake.

'My name's *Archie*,' said Archie.

'Ha ha! Of course it is. I felt I should apologise about our meeting the other day. So inconsiderate and insensitive of me! I thought it would be *lovely* if the twins came around to play, to get to know you better.'

'Great,' said Archie miserably. Mrs Puddingham-Pye wasn't the type to be sorry about anything and Archie could think of nothing worse than spending time with the Piglets. He didn't want to get to know them better than he already did, and he certainly couldn't trust them.

'What do you like to play?' he said, as the twins rolled out of the car.

'Hide-and-seek,' said Georgie immediately. Portia snorted.

'The hunter and the hunted,' remarked their mother, flashing a cold smile as she revved the engine. 'How thrilling! I can't wait to hear who triumphs.'

With a screech, the limousine drove off, leaving Archie to follow the twins inside.

'Fine,' he said as they stood in the hallway. 'Hide-and-seek it is. You hide, I'll seek.' The twins scampered off in different directions whilst he counted down from one hundred. If he was lucky they'd find an old dungeon and lock themselves in it.

'... Two ... one – ready or not, here I come!' he called. He opened the first door in the hallway. Behind it was a room that was more of a wide passageway, its walls covered in paintings and lined with suits of armour, tapestries and statues. There was no sign of a Piglet. A draught made the cobwebs hanging from the chandelier overhead tremble and Archie saw a familiar piece of paper gently sail into the room, coming to rest on the top of a statue. The magic letter! The next clue was here already – and he would have to solve it by himself!

Archie tiptoed into the room, scared he might disturb the people whose portraits hung on the walls around him. *They must be the McBudge ancestors*, he thought, studying the faces of the men and women from years gone by. They were all very grand in their fine clothes. Had they had to prove themselves worthy of the family name? One painting of a gruff-looking man with a magnificent beard caught his eye in particular. It was labelled *Gregor McBudge, Clan Chief*.

'Maybe one day I'll have a portrait of my own to sit alongside you,' he whispered. Gregor McBudge stared back silently.

Hanging on the wall in the centre of the room was a picture with the title *The Coat of Arms of the Clan Chief of the McBudges*. There was the shield with the castle tower on it, just like on the ring, flanked on either side by the now familiar dragons. Above the shield curled a motto with the words *DE ORE DRACONIS* written on it. What did that mean?

DE ORE DRACONIS

THE COAT OF ARMS
OF THE CLAN CHIEF OF
THE McBUDGE

Archie glanced at the magic letter in the
hope it might provide a clue. It still sat on top
of the statue, another dragon whose face was
frozen into a snarl. There was something strange about
the little metal statue standing on its pedestal, but Archie
couldn't quite put his finger on it. Anyway, the letter
wasn't telling, and he had neither Fliss's cleverness nor
Billy's wyrdie-facts to help him, just his own brain cells.

'Let's be logical,' he said to himself. The entire room
was devoted to the McBudge family. The clue must relate
to that somehow. Maybe Archie could find some helpful
information in the library. Tablet had mentioned that
there were books on the family's history in there.

He turned to run back into the hallway but stopped in his tracks. A suit of black armour stood as if to guard the door, the grim figure clutching a formidable axe in a gauntlet-covered hand. Archie watched, mesmerised, as its fingers twitched into life and its arm slowly raised the axe. With a lunge it hurled the weapon straight at him …

16

Archie just had time to jump sideways as the axe dropped towards him, its blade slicing through the air. It hit the floor behind him with a heavy thud.

'Oh, sorry,' said Portia, stepping out from her hiding place behind the armour, where she'd been covered by a tapestry. She looked rather disappointed. 'What a *terrible* accident. I can't think *how* that happened.'

Archie had almost forgotten the Piglets.

'You *threw* that!' he said angrily. 'You had your arm inside that suit of armour. It was deliberate.'

Portia strolled up to him casually and pushed her face close to his until they were eye-to-piggy-eye. Her sweaty breath formed an oily slick on his skin.

'Prove it!' she hissed. 'This old house is so old and

unsafe, I'm sure accidents happen all the time. You should be careful, or something *awful* might occur.'

'I've had enough of this game,' said Archie, pulling away. 'Let's find your brother so I've got you both where I can see you. I think I heard him go into the library.'

Portia hasn't noticed the letter, he thought, glancing with relief at the statue on whose head it still sat, *or she would have said something*. Goodness knows what would happen if the Puddingham-Pyes knew about his quest! The girl gave him a surly pout but followed him out of the portrait room and across the hallway.

Even though he hadn't been living long in the Hall, Archie had decided that the library was his favourite room. There was something comforting about all the books and the old sofa in front of the fire-place. He also liked the thought that Great-Uncle Archibald was keeping an eye on him from his painting up on the wall.

'What a *dump*!' said Portia, turning up her nose at the rows of ancient leather-bound volumes. If she hated it then Archie liked the library all the more.

'You look over there,' he said, walking over to the wall that was covered in bookcases. 'And I'll look over here.' Portia gave him a dismissive sniff and made a show of searching for Georgie in ridiculous places, lifting up cushions and peering in the wastepaper basket.

'Brother, dear!' she trilled. 'Where are yooou?' Meanwhile, Archie quickly scanned the shelves. There were all kinds of books on all kinds of subjects. There were the obvious sweet-related books: *The History of the Cocoa Bean and its Cultivation*, *My Life in Fondant – A Chocolatier's Story*, and *One Thousand Things to Do with a Walnut Whirl* amongst others. Then there was a bookcase with very deep shelves that was filled with giant atlases and charts. It also had some huge, thick books about the McBudge clan. There was *The Very Spooky Legend of Black Douglas McBudge*, *The McBudges of Dundoodle and Duntootie and their Family Connections*, and *The Cursed Jewels of Lady Deirdre Pookie*, but nothing that Archie thought might actually be useful.

'What are you looking at?' said Portia, bored with hunting for Georgie. 'Let me see!' She pushed Archie out of the way, knocking him over.

'Hey!' he said. 'Look out!' The girl stood over him, smirking. Then a shadow fell across them both, and Archie saw one of the massive books slowly edging itself off the shelf above them.

'No, really – LOOK OUT!' he called, rolling to one

side, but it was too late for Portia. The book tumbled from the shelf and she just had time to give a piggy squeal before it flattened her with a *CRASH!* She sprawled on the floor, wriggling like an upturned beetle under the weight of hundreds of ancient, dusty pages.

'Get it off me!' she wailed.

'Oops, sorry, sis.' Georgie peered out from the book-shelf overhead, looking sheepish. 'Didn't see you there.'

He clambered down from his hiding place and dragged the book off his slightly crushed, but none the worse, sister.

'I want to get out of this horrible place and go home!' she cried. 'Now!'

'But Mummy said –' began Georgie.

'NOW!' bellowed Portia, swatting at her brother. With a venomous glare at Archie, the twins stomped out of the library. He waited until he heard the front door slam behind them before chuckling with relief. That was a narrow escape – *two* narrow escapes, in fact! Archie went to pick up the book that had squashed Portia, which was still lying open. The pages were covered with curly writing and funny-looking pictures of people in strange clothes. But one picture made his eyes light up and his heart skipped a beat. It was *the McBudge coat of arms*!

Archie knelt on the floor, studying the words in front of him for clues. The book appeared to be telling the story of how the dragons ended up being part of the family crest.

> **And so the scribes tell**, Archie read, **that Gregor the Hairy, Clan Chief of the McBudges, chanced upon an injured dragon in the old forest of Dundoodle, not far from the fabled Wyrdie Tree. Being a man of honour, and not prone to needless violence in case it messed up his beard, Gregor nursed the noble beast until it was well enough to fly once more.**

'Good chief,' said the dragon, 'by your kindness you have shown yourself to have a heart warm enough to melt hard stone into golden honey. May your beard be ever coiffed! You and your family will be blessed by the dragons for evermore.'

And indeed good fortune fell upon the McBudge clan soon afterwards, so they took the dragon as their symbol and bore the motto DE ORE DRACONIS, *which means 'Out of the mouth of the dragon', for the dragon said it would be so.*

'Out of the mouth of the dragon,' Archie repeated. He was sure the family motto in the portrait room was a clue. It almost sounded like an instruction. But which dragon? And what was coming out of its mouth? Fire? Even Dundoodle couldn't be strange enough to have *real* dragons! Someone would have noticed great big fire-breathing lizards blundering around. The dragons on the roof of the Hall? No ... Archie jumped to his feet. Of course! The statue in the portrait room! It was the only dragon nearby, and that's where the letter had landed!

He raced back to the room, keeping clear of the suit of armour, just in case. The magical letter had vanished but that didn't deter him. He walked around the statue, searching for any secret hiding places. The dragon was made of a pale gold metal and was probably very heavy and valuable. Then Archie realised what had made the statue seem unusual earlier.

'There's *no* dust on it!' he said. Everything else in the room showed Tablet's trademark lack of housework skills but the dragon was *clean*. It must be new!

Archie carefully lifted the statue from its pedestal. To his surprise it weighed very little. It couldn't be metal after all. He scratched at the golden surface and almost

laughed as it snagged under his fingernail – it was metal foil! And underneath – dark, sweet-smelling chocolate! A hollow, chocolate dragon, like you might buy in a McBudge Fudge shop. He should have known – all the clues had *sweets* in them! He tore off the rest of the foil, grabbed the beast's nose and broke it away, scattering chocolate splinters over the floor.

'Out of the dragon's mouth,' he said, pulling a rolled-up strip of paper from inside the hollow creature. Archie unwound it between thumb and finger to find four words on it, written in caramel-brown ink:

MEMENTO MISERICORDIAE.
REMEMBER MERCY.

Archie tucked the mysterious message into his pocket and took the chocolate dragon back up to his bedroom where Sherbet was still snoozing, curled up into a bundle of white fur on the bed. He brought the wooden box out of his wardrobe and sat next to the dog, munching on chocolate dragon-snout and pondering the objects that had been collected so far.

There was the bell, the ring and now the message, as well as the plan of the unknown building, which was safely hidden in Fliss's secret den. The plan could be some kind of treasure map, but other than that it was all meaningless. Archie sighed.

'I hope one of the last two clues gets us an instruction

manual,' he said to Sherbet, who raised his head sleepily as Archie replaced the box in the wardrobe. 'Otherwise we're *never* going to complete this Quest. And that's if the Puddingham-Pyes don't get to me first ...'

Archie was still thinking about the baffling assortment of objects at breakfast the next morning. He and Mum had soon learned that the kitchen of Honeystone Hall was the best place for meals, partly because they hadn't yet found the dining room and Tablet seemed to have forgotten where it was (or even if they had one), but mostly because it was warm and inviting and always smelled of something delicious. The old butler really did know a thing or two about food, and how to keep a fire burning at a comfortable heat.

Whilst Archie devoured porridge, McBudge Velvetee Chocolate Fudge Spread on toast, and a big mug of tea, his mum told him about how her search for the missing secret ingredient was going. Badly, as it happened.

'I can't find *anything*,' Mum said. She wearily thumped her mug on the kitchen's oak table, making Sherbet jump up in panic from his bed on the floor nearby. 'It's very strange. I even found the original recipe for the first *ever* batch of McBudge Fudge. It has all the normal things you'd expect – milk, butter and sugar, but the only difference is that you have to add a teaspoon of powdered *dod* at the end.'

'Dod?' said Archie. 'What's that?'

'Precisely,' said Mum. 'I've never heard of it and I can't

find anything about dod in any books about food in the library, powdered or otherwise. It doesn't sound particularly tasty, whatever it is.'

'Indeed, Madam,' said Tablet, who was buttering some toast near the stove. 'It sounds like something the dog might have buried in the garden.' The butler gave one of his wheezing laughs, coughing so hard he let off a fart that rattled the teacups on the dresser.

Meanwhile, there was business to attend to.

'Mr Tatters is coming over for a meeting with some accountants,' said Mum. 'I've asked Mr Hankiecrust to attend. And I think you should come too, Archie. You're in charge, after all.'

They decided to have the meeting in the library. Mr Tatters arrived promptly, accompanied by two quiet, unsmiling men, called Mr Fade and Mr Fingers. Their pale skin merged with the drab grey of their suits, as if they were made from the same material. Mr Hankiecrust's friendly face was a very welcome addition.

'We've come up with a new sweet idea, Mr McBudge,' he whispered to Archie as they sat down around Great-Uncle Archibald's desk. 'Jelly Jumpers. They're a cross between jumping beans and jelly beans – sweets that you can bounce!'

He took a bean-shaped sweet from a pocket and flung it at the floor. It sprang back up off the wooden tiles, jumping so high it hit the ceiling, lodging in the crumbling old plaster above them.

'Some adjustment to the bounce may be required,' said Mr Hankiecrust, grinning awkwardly. 'I'll have to come back for that later.' Archie chuckled. He was glad someone normal was at the meeting.

Once everyone was seated, Mr Tatters spoke.

'As is usual when someone new takes over the reins of a business,' he said slightly nervously, 'I've asked Mr Fade and Mr Fingers of Fade, Fingers and Flint Accountants Limited to examine the accounts for the McBudge Fudge and Confectionery Company. I'm afraid they appear to have discovered some … discrepancies.'

'What kind of discrepancies?' said Mum, frowning at the grey men.

'You're asset-rich,' said Mr Fade.

'But cash-poor,' said Mr Fingers.

'What are they talking about?' said Archie. It didn't sound good whatever it was.

'You don't actually have any money,' explained Mr Tatters, looking flustered. 'The bank account is empty. Although you do own a lot of buildings and land. If something bad happened to the business then you might be forced to sell it all.'

Something bad, thought Archie. Like no one wanting to buy McBudge Fudge because it didn't have the secret ingredient that made it so delicious …

'Where did the money go?' said Mum. She looked shaken.

'Your great-uncle was a unique and eccentric individual,' said Mr Tatters, which Archie took to mean *completely bonkers*. 'It's unclear at the moment, but he seems to have just frittered the money away somehow. If you should have to sell the business I'm sure we could find a buyer. I've no doubt the Puddingham-Pyes would be interested. For the right price.'

'That's if I don't have an unfortunate accident in the meantime,' Archie muttered to himself.

After the lawyer and accountants had left, Archie and his mum discussed the latest discovery about dod with Mr Hankiecrust.

'We really need to find this dod, whatever it is,' the factory manager said. 'And soon! It's your only hope of saving the factory now.'

'We'll keep looking,' said Mum, her eyes alight with determination. 'This isn't just about us any more.

If the business is in trouble then so are lots of people's jobs.'

Coming to Dundoodle seemed to have given Mum a new lease of life. But Archie wasn't enjoying all this responsibility. Did he really want to finish this treasure hunt, if there was nothing left to inherit at the end of it? He looked up at the painting of Great-Uncle Archibald, scrutinising the old man's face. Why would he have gone to so much trouble to set up all these magical puzzles if it was all for nothing? Something wasn't right, Archie's instincts told him. And he was sure that the answer would lie at the end of the Quest. There was no choice. He *had* to continue.

19

With a new sense of purpose, Archie decided he would go and meet Fliss and Billy after school that afternoon, instead of waiting for them to come to the Hall. He hadn't seen much of Dundoodle, so it was a good chance to explore. He snapped Sherbet's lead on to the dog's collar and together they trudged into the cold afternoon air. The sky above them was like a bag of cotton wool about to burst: snow was on its way.

They had just got past the gates at the end of the drive when there was a flutter behind Archie's ear and the magical letter swept past, travelling at great speed. Sherbet strained at his lead, trying to chase the piece of paper and almost pulling the boy over.

'It's flying *away* from the Hall!' said Archie. 'That's odd. The next clue must be in the town.'

But the letter zigzagged around chimney pots and plunged between rooftops, taking an erratic course and flying far too quickly for them to follow.

'Why is it going so fast?' said Archie, his breath turning to steam as they ran to keep up with it. 'What's the hurry?' The reason soon became clear. As Sherbet dragged him down into the warren of streets, a small, dark shape zipped overhead like a hawk. The mobgoblin was back! There was evil intent in its movements. It was hunting the letter!

The chase was on. The letter ducked and dived, flapping its paper wings with all its might. The mob-goblin was bigger and ungainly but it shadowed the letter relentlessly, sometimes kicking its scaly feet against a chimney to give it an extra boost.

'Rip it! Shred it! Slice it!' the creature cackled.

Down below, Archie followed as best as he could, watching helplessly. Occasionally he lost sight of the race as it took him down back lanes where the eaves of houses cast sinister, jagged shadows, or twisted through roads where uneven cobbles seemed to trip him almost deliberately. Often he was so busy looking up that he bumped into passers-by, bouncing off their thick winter coats like a pinball and losing all sense of direction. But luckily Sherbet always knew which way to go.

Eventually they found themselves at the gates of Dundoodle School, just as its pupils were pouring out at the end of lessons. Fliss saw him and ran over, eager for news. Archie, out of breath, pointed upwards.

'If that thing gets the letter we'll never be able to complete the Quest!' he panted. Fliss stared as the letter circled the school, its little wings beating desperately. No one else seemed to notice – the letter was just litter fluttering about in the icy breeze. Billy appeared at their side, horrified at the sight of the mobgoblin swooping down on the defenceless piece of paper. It fled around the side of the school, into an empty alleyway. Fliss rummaged in her school bag as they dashed after it.

'I said we'd be ready for that thing the next time it showed up,' she said. 'And we are!' She pulled out a lollipop that was tied to a bundle of string.

'This is no time for a snack!' said Billy.

'That's rich, coming from you!' said Fliss. 'This is a McBudge Raspberry Slurpopop, as a matter of fact. Partially slurped. And it's not a snack, it's a weapon!'

Like a knife thrower at the circus, she aimed the

lollipop at the mobgoblin and then flung it as hard as she could. It soared through the air, trailing the tail of string behind it, and hit the little creature squarely in its fuzzy chest. The mobgoblin squeaked in surprise as the sticky sweet stuck fast to its skin. Fliss tugged on the other end of the string and reeled the creature in towards her as it bucked and struggled furiously, like a fish caught on a line.

'Let Garstigan go, horrid smellable little bratlings!' the mobgoblin rasped at them in a harsh voice. 'You are not Garstigan's keeper!'

Sherbet whined and growled, backing away in fear. Archie and Billy each grabbed the mobgoblin by its wings, whilst Fliss held on tightly to the string.

'Keep still, you little monster!' she said, as the creature wriggled in their hands. 'You're more slippery than an eel in a bowl of jelly!'

'The *keeper* is the mobgoblin's owner,' said Billy. 'Usually someone evil like a witch or a sorcerer or a dinner lady.'

'Who's your keeper?' Archie snapped at the creature. 'Who sent you to spy on me?'

'Garstigan will tell you *nothing*!' spat the mobgoblin. Archie tried again.

'You were trying to destroy my letter, Garstigan,' he said. 'Why?'

Garstigan's yellow eyes flashed but he didn't speak, he just watched as the letter flew down to earth, landing gently on the street nearby. With a sudden great effort, the mobgoblin pulled himself free of Billy's grasp, then bit through the string that anchored him to Fliss. He pushed his clawed feet into Archie's face and launched himself into the air, before diving back down on to the letter. Archie cried out in horror but it was too late. Garstigan ripped the paper to pieces, cackling spitefully. He took off once more and disappeared over the houses without a backwards look, the raspberry Slurpopop still stuck to his wiry little body.

'It's ruined,' said Archie, staring at the torn paper. He sank to his knees in despair. 'That's it. The Quest is over.'

20

The remains of the letter blew around Archie like snow-flakes. Just when he had finally been ready to rise to the challenge of the Quest, it had been taken away from him!

'What am I going to do?' he said, desperate tears forming in his eyes.

'There's only one thing to do at times like this,' said Fliss firmly. She pulled him to his feet. 'Have the biggest mug of hot chocolate we can find. With fudge marshmallows and caramel sprinkles. *And* white chocolate sauce on top!'

'Let's go to Clootie Dumpling's,' said Billy. 'Her hot chocolate is as dark as the soul of the Dark Lord of the bottomless Pit of Darquenesse – at midnight with the lights off!'

The two children steered Archie back through the streets towards the McBudge factory. Sherbet trotted behind, now and again glancing skywards, keeping watch in case the mobgoblin might decide to return. After a cold, silent walk, Archie found they had brought him to the McBudge Fudge shop.

Built on to the side of the factory wall, the shop sold all the sweets and chocolate made next door. A golden glow poured from its windows into the grey street, particularly welcome in the miserable twilit afternoon. Inside, the shop was a treasure trove of goodies, filled with talkative and boisterous children on their way home from school. They were noisily picking their favourite sweets from the vast selection the McBudge factory made, although the fudge was always the favourite. Some of them pointed at Archie as the three children entered, recognising him as the McBudge heir.

At the back of the shop was a little café that served tea, cake, sandwiches and other tasty things. Archie and the others sat themselves down at a quiet corner table near the kitchen, away from curious faces.

'Clootie Dumpling runs the café,' said Fliss lightly, as Sherbet curled up for a snooze under Archie's feet. 'She's got some witch-blood in her, I reckon.'

The little old lady who served them did indeed look like she might be just as at home stirring a cauldron as she was ladling hot chocolate into mugs. Her features were sharp but kindly, and a mound of white hair swept around her head, tied in a complicated plaited knot on top.

'It's lovely to meet you, young Mr McBudge,' said Clootie, as she brought the tray of hot chocolate over to their table. She looked at Archie with a sparkle in her eye. 'I've brought you some chewy fudge cookies too. You look like you've got a lot on your mind, and chewing always helps me think.'

'Chocolate always helps *me* think,' said Billy.

'Then you'll be a genius after you've downed this,' said Fliss, reaching for her mug. 'And we've got lots of thinking to do.'

Archie felt a lot better after a few sips of rich, sweet chocolate and the cheery, busy warmth of the café brought him out of his daze. But there was no escaping the gloomy facts.

'What now?' he said eventually. 'With no letter to lead us, how are we going to find the last two clues?'

'And to make things worse,' said Fliss. 'Someone out there wants to cause trouble. If Garstigan was sent to destroy the magic letter, then whoever sent him must know about the Quest.'

'He's been spying on you to see how far you've got,' agreed Billy. 'Remember how he was outside the window when you found the ring? So he knows you've got that, at least.'

'That means his keeper probably knows what the treasure is,' said Archie. 'And must want to stop us from getting it because it's important for something, and not just to prove that I'm worthy of the name McBudge.' He sighed thoughtfully and stared into his mug. 'But it doesn't matter anyway, now that I'm never going to find it.'

Just then Clootie returned to the table.

'It's very odd, Mr McBudge,' she said. 'But there's a letter here for you that appeared on the counter just now. I don't know who brought it – it must have flown in by itself!' She laughed and reached into an apron pocket, producing an envelope. It looked *very* familiar. All that was written on its front (in chocolate ink) were the words *ARCHIE McBUDGE*. The children glanced at each other, but didn't say a word until Clootie had gone back to the kitchen.

'Special delivery from spooky mail!' whispered Billy. 'The postal service of the dead is pretty efficient, I'll give them that.'

'A new letter to replace the old one!' said Archie, tearing at the envelope. He pulled out a folded piece of paper, a golden lollipop tumbling out on to the table with it. The lollipop was made of transparent, hard sugar, shaped into a circle, and glistened, like a honey-coloured jewel on the end of a white stick.

'It's a new clue!' said Archie. 'The Quest is back on!'

21

'That will do nicely as a replacement for the one that Garstigan has stuck to him,' said Fliss, picking up the lollipop and twirling it in her fingers. 'I wonder if he'll ever be able to unstick it?'

'What does the letter say, Archie?' said Billy. He slurped his hot chocolate impatiently, getting foamy marshmallow on the end of his nose.

'*Dear Archie,*' Archie read aloud. '*If you have received this letter then dark forces are at work to frustrate your cause. So it only seems fair that you should receive a little extra assistance. I hope this gift will help you see your path more clearly. Signed A. McB.*'

'Dark forces?' said Fliss. 'I don't like the sound of that.'

'*See your path more clearly* …' repeated Archie, his brow wrinkling. He put the letter safely into his coat pocket.

'Maybe the lollipop is a magic weapon,' suggested Billy. 'It burns with the phantom fire of the underworld to slice a path across a moonless graveyard, through the grasping hands of undead, maggot-infested corpses.'

'Will you stop with all the corpses and undeadness?' said Fliss, making a face and waggling the sweet at Billy. 'It's gross!'

The light from the kitchen shone through the glassy lollipop as Fliss waved it about her, making it glitter and flicker before Archie's eyes. He grabbed her wrist tightly and held her hand still.

'*Ow*!' said Fliss. 'You're hurting me!'

'Sorry – but look!' said Archie urgently. 'Look through the lollipop.'

He gently took the sweet out of Fliss's hand and held it in front of them. Fliss and Billy stared at the café through the golden pane of sugar-glass. The customers and shop workers, their sweets and clothes and faces, were all blurry and coloured a soft honey-brown, as might be expected. But around them, on the walls and the floor, and even the ceiling, were bright spots of light like little

specks of fire. When Archie took the lollipop away the fiery marks disappeared.

'It's like a magnifying glass!' said Billy. 'Dougie McFly in *Dougie McFly, Spectre Detector* uses one to search for clues.'

'But this one is showing things that are invisible!' said Fliss. 'What are those lights?'

Archie held the lollipop up to his eye and studied one of the marks on the near wall. It was round with five pointed lines coming away from its centre. It shone as if it were burning a hole through the wall.

'They're footprints!' he said. 'Tiny little footprints. Or paw prints perhaps. It's like something has been wandering all over the shop after stepping in glow-in-the-dark paint.'

'Rats!' said Fliss. 'Don't tell Clootie she's got magical rats.'

'They're too big to be rats,' said Billy expertly. 'They're claws. Mobgoblin tracks?'

'No,' said Archie firmly, shivering at the memory of

the long, knife-like feet that had scratched at his face earlier. 'Not a mobgoblin. There's one set of prints. I think it's another trail we have to follow.'

Trying not to attract too much attention, Archie wandered through the café and around the shop, the lollipop held close to his eye. Some of the other children gave him a strange look – the wealthy McBudge boy with his golden monocle – but he paid them no notice. The little feet led him to all corners of the room, sometimes doubling back on themselves, or walking in circles, or criss-crossing to make a knot of light like a nest of fire-flies. Eventually the trail traversed the floor and led under the door of the kitchen. Clootie was busy at the shop counter, packaging a chocolate box in shiny gift wrap for a customer.

'Cover me!' he whispered to Fliss and Billy who had been watching breathlessly. 'I'm going into the kitchen.'

'What if you meet … *whatever* it is that made the prints?' hissed Fliss, but Archie was already through the door.

The kitchen was empty. It was very tidy, with all the pots and pans and utensils hung across the wall on one side. Archie used the lollipop to follow the footprints around on what must have been quite an obstacle course for whatever little animal had made them. Behind jars of chocolate chips and fudge sprinkles it went, and in and out of boxes of marshmallows.

Finally they marched across the wall of kitchen equipment, passing metal spatulas and spoons, whisks and knives, stopping at what seemed to be a small silver hammer sitting alone on a shelf. A hammer in the shape of a *dragon*!

'It's amazing what one can find scurrying around a kitchen,' said a woman's voice from the doorway behind him. But it wasn't Clootie Dumpling. Mrs Puddingham-Pye loomed over him, a malicious glint in her eye.

22

'*What* are you up to, Urchin?' hissed the woman. She clutched her black handbag like a weapon. 'Your little friends outside tried to tell me you weren't in here but I saw you through the window.'

She sauntered towards him, a strange, sweet raspberry perfume wafting about her. Archie's heart beat like a drum. Had she seen him examining the dragon hammer?

'Were you admiring the kitchen tools?' continued the woman, running her finger along a rack of carving knives. 'So many *very* sharp objects. It's a wonder there aren't more terrible, *terrible* accidents. I'd be very careful if I were you, Urchin.' She picked a vicious-looking knife off the rack and, without even blinking, tossed it into the air so that it spun in a tight circle, before calmly catching it again by its handle. She fluttered her eyelashes at him innocently. *The P-Ps seem to be experts on accidents,* thought Archie with a shudder. He pulled himself together. There were too many people – too many witnesses – around for one of their 'accidents' to happen here.

'My name is Archie, not Urchin,' he said. 'This is *my* shop. Why shouldn't I be in here? The question is – what are *you* doing in here?'

Mrs Puddingham-Pye was taken aback for a moment. Then she smiled, resembling a shark Archie had seen in a nature documentary.

'Dear thing,' she purred, putting the knife back into the rack. 'I merely popped in to say that my darlings Georgie and Portia enjoyed playing with you *so* much that they couldn't *wait* for another attempt … er, visit, I mean. So I've just dropped them off at the Hall.'

Archie gulped. That was all he needed. He wasn't sure which was worse, being attacked by a flying demon or having to entertain the murderous twins again.

'They'll be waiting for you,' cooed Mrs Puddingham-Pye.

They're probably booby-trapping the front door right now, thought Archie. The woman glided back into the café, ignoring Fliss and Billy who were waiting nervously by the kitchen doorway. 'I hope you have a lovely, *lovely* time,' she called.

The two children hurried to Archie's side. He gave a long sigh of relief.

'I thought she was going to put me in the oven for a moment,' said Archie. 'She looks like the type of woman who might have a home in the forest made of gingerbread.'

'What weird thing did you find this time?' said Fliss. 'A metal detector made out of liquorice? A message written in marshmallows? A mime performed by jelly babies?'

Archie showed them the little silver hammer.

'It could be the mystical hammer of Throb, the god of headaches and family holidays,' said Billy, examining it reverently. 'Legend has it he lives on the top of Ben Doodle, along with Frij, the goddess of damp clothes, midges and leaky tents.'

Fliss rolled her eyes.

'You're the god of useless information, Billy,' she said. 'I'm beginning to wish I hadn't hired you.'

'You're only paying me in chocolate buttons,' muttered Billy.

'It's more like a toffee hammer,' said Archie, getting back to the matter in hand. 'I've seen them used in the factory to break up hard slabs of sugar. Let's put it with the other things.'

'We can go back to the Hall via the factory,' said Fliss. 'And pick up the toffee map from my secret hideout.'

'And that way we can sneak up on the Piglets,' said Archie. 'Before they sneak up on us.'

He stuffed the hammer into his coat pocket along with the letter, and they slipped back into the café. They woke Sherbet from his snooze and made their way quickly out on to the street and into the factory next door, slipping up some backstairs to the gangway where Fliss's den was hidden. They passed the burst sack of icing sugar, still lying where it had almost hit Archie a couple of days before.

'Nobody comes this way,' said Fliss. 'So it hasn't been tidied up yet.'

But somebody *had* been that way. There were footprints in the spilt icing sugar leading along the gangway towards the hideout. Fliss stopped suddenly. Her face was pale.

'Someone's been in there!' she whispered. The prints clearly led behind the maze of pipes that formed the entrance to the den.

'They might *still* be in there!' said Billy, but Fliss didn't wait. She clambered through the pipes before the boys could stop her. There was silence for a heartbeat.

Then Fliss's voice wailed eerily from behind the muddle of metalwork.

"It's gooooone!"

'What?' said Archie. They followed her into the hideout. She looked horrified. All her things had been thrown about. It was a complete mess. 'What's gone?' Archie repeated.

'The box,' said Fliss. 'The box with the toffee jigsaw, and Billy's drawing of the map. *It's been taken*!'

23

'From doom to joy and back to doom again,' said Billy, gravely surveying the wreck of the hideout. 'This Quest is turning into a real roller coaster!'

Fliss was furious. She kicked at an upturned stool.

'When I get my hands on whoever did this,' she said, picking up a spanner, 'I'll take them apart and put them back together with their bits all the wrong way around!'

It was Archie's turn to provide them with some cheer.

'We can soon tidy up,' he said. 'It will be as right as rain in no time. And as for the map, we know a person took it and not some magical creature. Those footprints are definitely human. That gives me some hope the map isn't lost for good. Let's get back home before anything else happens.'

They marched quickly to the passage that linked the factory to Honeystone Hall. Archie carefully checked for signs of the Piglets in the hallway of the house before they silently ran upstairs to his bedroom. They added the hammer to the box in the wardrobe and Archie showed them the strange message he had found inside the chocolate dragon.

'This is the weirdest assortment of stuff,' said Fliss. 'It's like the clutter I keep in my tool kit.'

'Anyone would think you were collecting for a car boot sale, not a treasure hunt,' said Billy. Archie nodded.

'The biggest test of this Quest is going to be working out what each thing is for,' he said. 'Whether we have a map or not.'

He put the wooden box safely back in the wardrobe. At that moment his coat, which he had dumped on the floor and which Sherbet was using as a bed, suddenly began to twitch as if it were coming to life. The dog jumped up and growled suspiciously.

'It's possessed!' gasped Billy. 'A laundry poltergeist – they usually go for underpants – a rating of four point nine on the Macabre Creepy Scale!'

'It's the *letter*,' said Archie. 'It's trying to get out of my pocket.' Sure enough the folded paper wiggled out from inside the coat and spread its crisp, white wings. It flapped towards Archie's bedroom door, where it hovered expectantly. Archie opened the door and the letter flew away down the corridor.

'The last clue!' said Fliss. 'Quick – after it!'

It was dark outside and the house was now filled with shadows. They stumbled down the passage and arrived at the top of the stairs as the letter swept down the stairwell. Billy was fastest and got there before the others, jumping down a couple of steps at a time, closely followed by Archie and Fliss. The letter floated into the hallway at the bottom, before diving through the open doors of the library. *The library is where it all started*, thought Archie. It was funny that the final clue should be in there.

Billy had just reached the top of the last flight when he tripped and went flying headlong. Archie scarcely managed to grab Billy's outflung arm before the boy plunged down the staircase. He clung to Archie in fright.

'That was close!' said Fliss. 'Be more careful, Billy! You could have damaged something important. Like the carpet.'

'I was tripped up!' said Billy angrily. 'And *not* by a poltergeist.' He pointed to his ankle. In the dim light they could just make out that it was caught by a length of

thread stretched across the stair.

'The Piglets!' said Archie. 'Another one of their death traps.'

'It almost worked too,' said Fliss. 'That's really creepy.'

'So creepy I'm ready to give them a rating on the Macabre Creepy Scale,' said Billy, his face burning. 'And maybe a Macabre Punch-On-Their-Noses for good measure.' Two faces appeared at the bottom of the stairs.

'Have a nice trip?' said Georgie, smiling wickedly. Portia giggled.

'I'll send *you* on a trip!' yelled Billy, charging down the

stairs. 'With a one-way ticket to *Kickinthepantsville*!'
Archie and Fliss stared at each other. They had never seen
Billy like this before. Neither had the twins, who hurriedly
retreated into the library in the face of the enraged boy,
slamming the doors behind them. Billy pounded his fists
against the heavy wooden entrance.

'We need to get in there,' said Archie. 'The last clue!'
He and Fliss joined Billy at the library doors. They leaned
against them and pushed with all their might. It was too
much for the Piglets, who staggered back from the
doorway as the others forced their way in.

'Keep away from us,' said Portia, running to the desk.
'Or ... or we'll eat all your chocolates.' She frantically
grabbed at an open box that was sitting on the desk. It
was chocolate – a box of McBudge Chokidigits, chocolate
shaped into numbers. Archie glanced at Fliss and Billy.
The magic letter was sitting next to the box, unnoticed
by the twins. The Chokidigits must be the final clue!

Archie made a dash for the desk but Georgie and
Portia's gluttonous faces meant business. He just got a
sight of the chocolates before they tumbled into the
twins' greedy mouths. The clue was gone forever.

24

'You snout-nosed, oily trough hogs!' Archie yelled. 'They weren't for you!'

'Who cares?' sneered Portia, her mouth all sticky. 'You've got loads of chocolate anyway.'

'Yeah,' said Georgie darkly. 'For now.'

Archie was seething. But not as much as Billy. Letting out a huge roar, he ran towards the twins, chasing them around the table and out of the library. They fled squealing, terrified by the strange boy's rage. Fliss quickly shut the library doors behind them, then Billy and Archie pushed a heavy armchair against the doors to stop them coming back in.

'You were very impressive,' Fliss said to Billy as he slumped in the chair. 'You were like a possessed wrath-monster. Fliss rating – ten out of ten.' Billy chuckled.

'I enjoyed that,' he said. 'And at least it's got rid of them for a while.'

'It doesn't matter,' sighed Archie. 'It's too late! Those horrors have eaten the clue.'

'We can't give up now!' said Fliss. 'Not after everything else we've been through.'

'Think, man!' said Billy. 'You were closest to the chocolates. What did you see?'

Archie racked his brains.

'There were only three chocolates,' he said. 'They were lined up in a row.'

'What numbers were they?' said Fliss. 'Try and remember, Archie!'

Archie concentrated. He could see in his mind Portia grabbing the box and tipping the chocolates out.

'A four, a two …' He could see Portia trying to get the last chocolate before her brother, her fat little hand desperately reaching for … a three? 'No, wait – an eight!' he said. 'A four, a two and an eight! I remember!'

'Well done, Archie!' said Fliss. She frowned. 'But what does that mean?'

'It could be part of a spell or incantation,' said Billy, scratching his chin. 'They often invoke the arcane science of Numerology. Or it could be the phone number of McGreasy's Pizza Delivery.'

'Or the combination of a safe,' said Fliss. 'Or maybe coordinates on a map – they're made up of numbers.'

'There are several books of maps in here,' said Archie. 'I saw them when we were playing hide-and-seek the other day.' He walked alongside the wall of bookshelves. 'Let's see – there was one on the fifth bookcase, third shelf up, about the sixth book along …' He stopped.

'What?' said Fliss. 'What's the matter?'

'That's it!' said Archie, grinning. 'It's not a map coordinate, it's a book location. That's why the chocolates were left in the *library*. Four, two, eight – fourth bookcase, second shelf up, eighth book along!'

They ran over to the fourth of the many bookshelves, counting two rows up and then along the shelf to the eighth book. Archie pulled the book from the shelf and read the cover.

'*The Insect Life of Loch Flicmaibogie*,' he said. 'By Fraser Dripping-Tingle.

'That doesn't sound promising,' said Billy. Archie flicked through the pages.

'It's just a book about gnats,' he said, disappointed. 'Lots of them. Could this be the object we're meant to find?' They crowded around the book, hoping for inspiration.

'Hang on,' said Fliss suddenly. 'Maybe it's second shelf *down*, not up.' She clambered up a stepladder to the second shelf down and picked out the eighth book.

'*Dreadful Desserts, Sweets for the Creatures of the Otherworld*, by F. Bixington,' she said, carefully carrying the thick book back down the ladder. 'That's more like it! *Hmmm* … it's much lighter than it looks.'

Archie opened the book on the desk. His eyes lit up.

'Brilliant, Fliss!' he said. 'It's not a book – it's a box *disguised* as a book! The pages aren't real.' The others peered into the fake book to see three more Chokidigit numbers hidden inside.

'Seven, four, two,' said Fliss. 'Another book location?' Billy got to the seventh bookcase first and found the corresponding volume.

'*Scrumtastic Feasts and Where to Find Them*,' he read. It was another fake book with another set of chocolate numbers.

'This is a great way to hide chocolates from you, greedy-guts,' said Fliss as Billy munched on the discarded numbers. 'Honestly – you're not so much Billy Macabre as Billy Ma*carbohydrate*.' Meanwhile, Archie had found the next book.

'*Ali Baba and the Forty Thieves*,' he read, looking at the gold letters printed on its spine. 'Odd. It's not sweet-related.' He pulled at the book on its shelf but it stuck. 'It won't come out,' he said. Just then, there was a quiet *click* from behind the bookcase and it slowly swung away from the wall. Billy whistled.

'Open Sesame!' he said. 'A real-life secret passage! This place really does have it all.'

Behind the bookcase there was a doorway, with stone steps leading down into the gloom below. There were scratching noises and the smell of damp air wafted upwards. It didn't look very inviting.

'That looks really eerie,' said Fliss. 'Like *Tunnel of the Slime Zombies*-eerie.'

'Slime zombies live in sewers and drains,' Billy corrected her. 'This is much more were-slug territory.'

Sherbet barked a warning – there were scuffling noises from the other side of the doors. It was the twins!

'Let us in!' called Georgie. 'Or we'll tell Mummy you've been horrible to us!' The doors pushed against the chair as the Puddingham-Pyes tried to batter their way through.

'Were-slugs or the Piglets?' said Archie, grabbing the letter and stuffing it in his pocket. 'It's not much of a choice – come on!'

He scrambled through the doorway, Fliss, Billy and Sherbet following after. They just got the bookcase shut behind them before they heard the sound of the twins bursting into the library. They would have a surprise! But now there was only one way out. Archie stepped into the darkness.

25

They carefully made their way down the tunnel. It was very difficult to see.

'We're right underground,' whispered Fliss, shivering in the cold. 'I wonder where it leads.'

They didn't have long to find out. The tunnel brightened suddenly, illuminated by many candles stuck into alcoves in the stone walls, pale stalagmites shaped by years of melted, dripping wax. They could hear the sound of lapping water ahead. Eventually the tunnel opened out into a small cave, rippling shadows playing across its arched roof. By the flicker of a single lantern hanging from a hook on the wall they could see the ground formed a pebble shore that fell away into water: the loch, an expanse of inky black under the night sky.

'The passage is a secret way to get to the loch from Honeystone Hall!' said Archie.

'I've been out on the loch before and I've never seen this cave,' said Billy. 'It must be well hidden from the rest of Dundoodle.'

They trudged over to the shoreline. Outside the cave, snowflakes began to fall gently.

'There's no other exit,' Fliss observed, kicking a pebble into the water. 'We're stuck until the twins decide to go home. Unless a boat passes by.'

Archie looked around.

'I was expecting to find something here,' he said. 'All the other clues have led to an object of some kind.' They began to search amongst the rocks, looking for boxes, treasure chests or scrolls or anything out of place. Even Sherbet joined in, sniffing in every nook and crevice.

'If only I'd brought my torch,' said Fliss. 'It's difficult to see by the light of that stupid lamp.'

Archie glanced at the small lantern. It was odd that it was the only light in the cave when the tunnel had been filled with candles. Its flame seemed unnatural too. He walked over to the wall where it hung to get a better look. The lamp was made of a silvery metal, decorated with leaves and flowers in swirling patterns. Inside wasn't a candle, but a gemstone, a golden crystal that appeared to float inside the lamp. The light came from an unearthly, wispy flame that was trapped behind the crystal's faceted surface.

'It's the lantern!' he said. '*This* is what we're supposed to find.' The others hurried to his side.

'I've read about these,' said Billy, his big eyes looking owlish in the lamp's strange glow. 'Wyrdie-lights.'

'It's beautiful,' gasped Fliss. 'Please tell me this isn't some undead corpse-y thing.'

'It's a living fire that has no fuel but burns forever,' Billy replied, gazing in fascination. 'The crystal stops it from escaping.'

'We probably ought to leave it here,' said Archie. 'I'm

not sure anywhere in the Hall is secure enough after today. In fact, I think I'll bring the box with the other finds down here for safe keeping.'

As they left the cave, Archie noticed another empty alcove in its rocky wall. A silver hook embedded into the stone caught his eye. Something was obviously meant to hang from the hook in that alcove. Another lantern? Suspended from a chain underneath the niche was a tiny hammer, much smaller than the one he had found in Clootie's kitchen. Archie's mind began to race as they plodded back up through the tunnel. Ideas were forming. Pieces were falling into possible places ...

His thoughts were interrupted by their arrival at the doorway into the library. All was quiet.

'The twins must have got bored and left,' whispered Fliss. Archie pushed the back of the bookcase and it slowly opened. They stepped back into the warmth and light of the library.

'So *that's* where you were hiding,' came a sneer from an armchair. It was Mrs Puddingham-Pye.

26

Archie gasped. Mrs Puddingham-Pye was the last person he wanted to see. She leaped from her chair with the speed of a cat. Luckily, Fliss had the good sense to slam the bookcase back into place before Mrs Puddingham-Pye could glimpse what was behind it.

'What's in there?' the woman spat, her claw-like fingers gripping the bookcase and shaking it frantically. 'How do you open it? Tell me, Urchin!'

'Try "Open Sesame",' said Archie slyly. 'And it's none of your business anyway. This is *my* house.' Mrs Puddingham-Pye growled.

'You impudent little brat …' she began, but just then Mum walked in carrying a tray with a teapot and teacups. '… who's so full of fun and games! *Delightful* child.' She patted Archie on the head and sat back in the armchair like a hunched spider, her handbag planted by her side on the floor.

'*There* you are, Archie!' said Mum, putting down the tray and pouring the tea. 'Cousin Jacqui has come to pick up the twins. They've been looking all over for you. Tablet has had to entertain them.'

'Poor Tablet!' said Archie. 'Do we need to call an ambulance?'

Mrs Puddingham-Pye ignored him and sipped her tea daintily.

'A little bird tells me that all is not well at the factory,' she said, raising her painted eyebrows inquisitively. 'There's talk in the town that a certain secret ingredient is proving *so* secretive that nobody can *find* it.' She gave a short little laugh. 'Naughty little ingredient!'

'Really?' said Mum, flustered. She and Archie exchanged glances.

'A terrible tragedy *if* it were true!' said Mrs Puddingham-Pye. 'It would be a *catastrophe* for McBudge Fudge and Dundoodle. Maybe the factory would have to close!' She widened her eyes dramatically at the thought. 'Of course, if the worst *did* happen, Tosh and I would be helpful in *any* way we could.' *Helpful like the big, bad wolf was helpful to Little Red Riding Hood*, thought Archie.

'We know exactly where the naughty little ingredient is,' he said. 'You shouldn't listen to rumour.' Why did he say that? He hadn't a clue where it was! Mrs Puddingham-Pye stared at him as if she were trying to prise open his brain with her eyes.

'How simply wonderful!' she said. 'Gossip is a *terrible* thing. I'm always as quiet as the grave, myself.'

'Actually, graves aren't very quiet,' put in Billy. 'What with all the munching from twelve different types of maggots and the tormented wails of the undead, but we know what you mean.' Mrs Puddingham-Pye looked at Billy like he was an insect she had found swimming in her teacup.

'Peculiar boy,' she said. 'What strange company you keep, young Urchin!' She quickly finished her tea. 'Now, this has been *lovely* but I must be on my way.'

With a barked 'CHILDREN!' she summoned Georgie and Portia from the hallway, where they had been drawing all over a dozing Tablet's face. She picked up her handbag from the floor – wait, had it moved? Archie was sure it had been closer to her chair – and strode out of the Hall, her odd raspberry perfume lingering long after the front door had shut behind them.

'What made you say that?' said Mum, clearing up the tea things. 'We still don't know where this dod ingredient thing is.'

'I can't stand seeing her so smug,' said Archie. 'She might be family, but she's no friend, Mum.' Mum sighed and shook her head.

'It's getting late,' she said, carrying the tea tray out of the library. 'Time you kids were getting back to your own homes.'

'We'll see you back here after school tomorrow,' whispered Fliss, as she and Billy plodded out into the dark, snowy night. Archie nodded. It had been a busy day and there was lots to talk about.

That night Archie slept fitfully, even though Sherbet had crept on to his bed to make it extra warm and toasty. His mind kept running through the list of things they had found, trying to find some kind of pattern. But none materialised. It was just a clutter of random objects, like Fliss's tool kit. *Like Fliss's tool kit …*

There was a *THUD*. Was Mum up? Was Tablet sleep-walking like last night? They had found him in the bath wearing only a woolly hat and muttering 'Parsnips!'

Archie jumped out of bed and tiptoed downstairs. Sherbet accompanied him, staying close to his heels. The dog sniffed the air and growled.

'Quiet,' Archie hissed. 'We don't want to wake anyone.' The doors to the library were open. He could hear scuffling sounds coming from inside. Archie peered around the doorway, his heart beating fast. There amongst the shadows, another darker shadow moved stealthily. Someone was in there and they didn't want to be seen!

27

Sherbet dived into the room, barking furiously at the intruder.

'No, Sherbet!' cried Archie. 'Come back!'

The shadow froze for a moment then sprang towards the window. It was attempting to make its escape! Sherbet chased after it but Archie made a grab for his collar, not wanting the brave little dog to get hurt. He flicked the switch of a nearby table lamp just as the intruder lunged at the long, heavy curtain that hung over the library window. The bat-like shape was unmistakable: it was Garstigan!

The monster snarled down at him as its bony claws gripped and shredded the thick material, just out of Archie's reach.

'Can't catch Garstigan, stinky bratling!' it gurgled merrily. 'No sticky sweeties this time!' Traces of Fliss's Slurpopop were still stuck to the mobgoblin's body, the sickly, fruity smell of the lollipop overpowering the library's usual smell of leather, wood and dust. Where had Archie smelled that before? Books lay on the floor in heaps, thrown from the bookcase that hid the secret passage. That must have been the thud Archie had heard. The creature had been trying to find the hidden door! Luckily the *Ali Baba* book was still in its place.

Sherbet wriggled free from Archie's grasp and jumped at Garstigan, who leaped from the curtain with a squawk and flapped out of the open window. Archie ran over to it, snowflakes blowing into his face, to see the mobgoblin fly to the side of a figure silhouetted against the white blanket that now formed the garden. He could only just make out who the person was in the darkness, but the large handbag would have given them away in any case: *it was Mrs Puddingham-Pye!* She was Garstigan's keeper!

The creature crawled inside the handbag and the figure trudged quickly away from the Hall. That's why she had smelled of raspberries: she had Garstigan hiding in her handbag the whole time. He must have let

himself out and hidden when she came to pick up the twins. That would explain how the handbag had moved!

He made sure the window was properly shut, then quickly returned all the books to their places on the shelves. What if Mrs Puddingham-Pye decided to try again that night? There was no way he was going to be able to sleep after that, so he might as well guard the secret passage as best as he could. He curled up on the sofa and, cuddling Sherbet for warmth, went over everything that had happened since he had first arrived in Dundoodle. He was still thinking when the sky lightened behind the curtains and the snow-covered world outside was revealed.

After a bleary-eyed breakfast, he was surprised to find Fliss and Billy knocking at the front door, bundled up in heavy coats and scarves and stamping snow from their boots.

'School's closed!' said Fliss, marching gleefully into the hallway. 'The pipes have burst so there's no heating. If we're lucky it won't reopen until after Christmas.'

'I've some news of my own!' said Archie. The two children warmed themselves up in front of the roaring library fire as he told them what had happened.

'Mrs P-P is the keeper?' said Billy, astonished. 'That means she must be some kind of witch. Or know something about magic.'

'I've been thinking about that, amongst other things,' said Archie. 'Great-Uncle Archibald must have known about magic, and they're both McBudges. Maybe there's magic running in the family.'

'It also means she's the one who's trying to stop you completing the Quest,' said Fliss, tickling Sherbet's ears. 'Whatever we're looking for, she doesn't want you to get it. I bet she stole the map from my hideout!'

Billy perked up at the mention of the map.

'That reminds me!' he said. 'I knew I'd seen that building plan before.' He rummaged in his black bag and dragged out a folder bound with an elastic band. 'During my research on wyrdie-related places in Dundoodle, I found this in the school library.' He began to flick through the yellowed pages of the folder as the others looked on curiously. 'Years ago, some pupils did a project on local buildings and landmarks, finding out about their history, making drawings of them, that kind of thing. They even made plans of the rooms in the buildings using information from historical documents.'

'Did you find *our* building?' said Fliss excitedly. 'If you have, then we don't need to worry about the stolen map.'

'I did,' grinned Billy. 'And you'll never guess where it is …'

'I will,' said Archie. 'It's Pookiecrag Castle.'

28

'You're right!' said Billy, slightly deflated.

'Pookiecrag Castle?' squealed Fliss. 'The most haunted place in Dundoodle?'

'*Nobody* goes there,' said Billy. 'It rates nine point eight on the Macabre Creepy Scale – just below Auntie Doreen and her moustache.'

'Nobody goes there *except* a true McBudge,' said Archie, 'and I have the Ring of the McBudges.' He had brought the wooden box belonging to his dad out from its hide-away in the wardrobe and placed it on his great-uncle's desk that morning. Opening it now, he laid out each of the items they had found on the desk's leather-lined surface.

'Do you think that's what you're supposed to do?' asked Fliss, joining him at the desk. 'Travel to the castle?'

Archie nodded.

'Yesterday you said that the things we had collected reminded you of your tool kit. I think that's exactly what this is – a tool kit to help us find the treasure.'

'Do you know what each object is for?' said Billy, turning over the scrap of paper with the peculiar words on it.

'No,' Archie admitted. 'But I've an idea of where to start. And I've an idea what the treasure is too.'

'What?' said Fliss eagerly. 'Gold? Diamonds?'

'Or an enchanted amulet?' said Billy hopefully. 'One that grants the power to cross over into the nether realm and converse with the spirits of the ancient druids?'

'No, no,' said Archie. 'And *no*. I have to prove I'm worthy of the name McBudge, worthy to carry on the business. In the last few days I've learned that the McBudge business relies almost entirely on one thing.'

'The secret ingredient!' said Fliss. '*That's* the treasure!'

'There's no trace of it anywhere in the Hall or the factory,' said Archie, replacing all the items in the box. 'But where better to hide this really valuable dod stuff than the one place *no one* will go – Pookiecrag Castle. Remember how the golden Dragum pointed to it?'

'I still like my amulet idea better,' said Billy. 'But if the treasure is "dod" then I can see why Mrs P-P would want to stop you finishing the Quest. Without the ingredient, the McBudge business falls apart. Then she's ready to buy it up cheaply.'

'And if she gets her hands on the secret ingredient later,' said Archie, 'she can get the business going again and make a tidy profit.'

'But Pookiecrag Castle island is on the other side of the loch,' Fliss pointed out. 'How do we even get there? All the paths are blocked by snow and it's not like there's a bridge.'

Archie tucked the box under his arm. Walking over to the bookcase, he tugged the copy of *Ali Baba and the Forty Thieves*, opening the secret passage. 'We have our own personal entrance to the loch,' he said. 'I've a hunch we'll find our transport nearby.' As he entered the hidden doorway he glanced at the painting above the fireplace. Was that a smile he saw on the face of his great-uncle?

Fliss and Billy were uneasy, but grabbed their coats and followed him down the steps of the shadow-filled tunnel, with Sherbet trotting behind. In the cave, the wyrdie-lantern still shone from its place on the wall. Ice encrusted the edges of the loch, which was veiled in a silvery mist.

Archie placed the box on the stone floor and opened the lid.

'The first thing we found was the bell,' he said, taking it out and holding it up to the light. 'I think it's the first part of the tool kit we have to use.' They watched as he carried it over to the empty alcove he had noticed the day before. The bell had a metal loop on its top, which fitted neatly over the hook. Archie picked up the tiny hammer that hung from the chain beneath the alcove.

'Do you think you should ring it?' said Billy. 'You could be summoning Saggie Aggie, the mermaid of the loch. Macabre Creepy Scale rating of seven. She's supposed to be so old her hair's all fallen out so she uses her comb to scratch her scaly bum.'

'It's what I have to do,' said Archie. 'I just know it.'

He tapped the bell gently with the hammer and it vibrated with a clear note.

They waited. Nothing happened. No elderly, bald mermaid appeared. There was silence.

Then, from the distant shore, where they knew the castle lay hidden behind the wraith-like mist, a dark shape appeared, gliding through the water.

'Look!' said Fliss, pointing at the loch. 'Something's coming towards us.'

It was a small boat. There was no doubt it was heading straight for them, its dragon-headed prow glaring at them fearsomely.

'Who's steering it?' said Archie. 'There's no one aboard!'

'It could be the dreaded invisible oarsmen of the Viking ghost ship of the Fjord of Fjurge!' warned Billy. 'They used to raid these parts over a thousand years ago.'

The mysterious empty boat gently came to rest on the beach. Sherbet growled but no ghostly Vikings appeared. The children approached it cautiously.

'It's like it's waiting for us,' said Archie.

Fliss rapped the sides of the boat with her knuckles, testing for a concealed engine.

'Maybe it's remote-controlled,' she said.

'No,' said Archie, running his hand over the boat's carved dragon's head. 'There's no machinery in here at all. This is *magic*. This is how we'll get to the castle.'

'Do you *really* want to go?' said Billy. He looked at them anxiously.

'Yes,' said Archie. 'I've never been so sure of anything.' The end of the Quest – and the end of the factory's troubles – could be in sight.

Archie removed the wyrdie-light lantern from the wall and placed it and the box into the boat. Then they clambered inside. Sherbet whined, unsure of the strange craft.

'How do we make it move?' asked Fliss. As if in answer, the boat slid smoothly into the loch and was swallowed up by the mist. It cut through the gloomy water, picking up speed as it went. The children clung tightly on to its sides as the frosty air churned around them. Archie held up the lantern to see better, but the mist was too thick. However, its golden light helped to soothe their nerves and keep their spirits up, as they made their hushed journey.

Eventually the jagged towers of the castle emerged from the haze in front of them. The boat navigated a course for itself through a labyrinth of sharp rocks that jutted from the water like teeth, and drew alongside a snow-covered stone quay.

But theirs wasn't the only boat moored by the castle. Someone else had got there first.

30

'It must be Mrs Puddingham-Pye!' whispered Fliss. 'She's beaten us to it!'

They scrambled out on to the quay, warily approaching the motorboat. It was empty. Fresh footprints led away towards the silent, threatening walls of the castle.

'These are the same footprints as those we found in the factory,' said Billy, as Sherbet sniffed around the flattened snow. 'So she's the one who stole the map!'

'What shall we do?' said Fliss.

'We go on,' said Archie. 'She might have the map but she doesn't have the rest of the tool kit. And there's three of us and one of her.'

'She's got her flying monkey as well, don't forget,' said Fliss.

'And we've got Sherbet,' said Archie. The dog wagged its stubby tail determinedly.

Archie tucked the box under his arm and held up the lantern to light their way in the mist, as they trudged towards the castle's crumbled gates. A cold wind moaned through the skeletal building, its doleful ruins smothered with frostbitten ivy. There were no lights in any of the windows and no signs of life of any kind. But the place had a feeling of watchfulness, just like Archie had noticed when he had first arrived at Honeystone Hall.

'If a wolf were to howl right now I would probably wet myself,' said Billy in a slightly strangled voice. 'I just thought I'd warn you.'

'You're supposed to be the *expert* on creepiness!' hissed Fliss.

'We were meant to come here,' said Archie firmly. 'We mustn't be afraid. But we must be quiet and watch out! Mrs P-P is in there somewhere …'

They stepped through fallen doorways, and slipped and slid over tumbled walls and stairs, the stones slick with moss and ice. It was hard work. The snow was patchy inside the castle and they soon lost the trail of footprints. Billy's chilled hands held the old hand-drawn map up to the lantern's light.

'Do you know where we are?' asked Fliss. 'It feels like we're walking in circles.'

'The stolen map had a dragon on it,' Billy said, 'which pointed to a room in the centre of the castle. But the castle's so ruined it's hard to tell where one room starts and another finishes. It's just a great big frozen pile of spooky rubble.'

'We can't give up,' said Archie. 'Let's try and head to the middle and see what we find.'

They followed a passage that led under a grand arch and into a wide hall, open to the heavy sky. More snow was on its way. A massive stone fireplace was slumped against one wall, the broad chimney breast reaching to where the roof had once been, like the crooked backbone of a giant.

'I think this is it,' said Billy. 'This was the room the dragon was pointing at.' Archie glanced at the map. Something on the page caught his attention. He was about to speak when Fliss grabbed his arm.

'Look at the sky!' she said. 'What's *that*?'

At first Archie thought they were shooting stars:

fast-moving smudges of light leaving fiery trails through the clouds. But it was still daylight, and these stars moved in formation like a flock of birds, now diving downwards towards the castle. The glowing fireballs swept into the hall, circling the room several times, and buzzing past the astonished children. They weaved in and out of the tumbledown walls and doorways, lighting up the stonework so that spiked shadows danced about the ruins. More and more of the little comet-like objects followed, a swarm of living fireworks.

Archie and the others looked on, both amazed and delighted. One smaller fireball paused by the children for a moment, as if to inspect them, before chasing after the others. All at once they launched themselves into the sky, before turning back towards the earth and plummeting down the chimney, one after the other. The children saw that the stone hearth had opened – there was a hidden trapdoor in the floor of the fireplace! The procession of fireballs funnelled out of the bottom of the chimney, into the fireplace and straight through the trapdoor, disappearing into the gloom underground. With the last one through, the trapdoor shut with a heavy *clunk* and the castle fell once more into its watchful half-light, leaving them with only the glimmer from Archie's lantern.

'Did you see?' said Fliss, turning to face the boys and breathless with excitement. 'Did you SEE?'

'Yes,' said Archie, his eyes shining. '*Dragons*. Lots and lots of little *dragons*!'

31

'The legends about Pookiecrag Castle were true!' said Billy, as they scrambled over to the fireplace. 'It *is* haunted by flickering shapes – but not ghosts. Dragons!'

'They weren't any bigger than kittens,' said Fliss. 'Not what I expected dragons to look like at all. They looked … cute.'

'Dragons are everywhere in McBudge history,' said Archie. 'Now we know why. The dragon on the map pointed here, to the fireplace. We have to follow them!'

Billy stamped on the hearth. It looked solid and certainly wasn't going to move easily.

'You must need to use something from the tool kit!' he said. 'Perhaps the hammer?'

Archie shook his head. The hammer was tiny – it

would never work against these large flagstones. He waved the lantern over the chimney breast. It had been carved with shapes and patterns: dragons and plants snaked over the canopy, drawing Archie's eye along with them. The twisting design focused on a single point, a small circle cut deeply into the stone.

'Look at this,' he said. The circle contained an image they all recognised.

'A tower on a shield,' said Fliss. 'The McBudge crest that's on all the packets of McBudge Fudge. And on that ring we found.'

Archie took the Ring of the McBudges from the box.

'The circle in the wall is the same size,' he said, placing the ring into it. 'They were made to fit.' As soon as the metal touched the stone, they heard a soft scraping sound from the ground beneath them. A flagstone in the hearth slowly moved aside, revealing a pitch-black tunnel below, accessed by some worn steps.

'This is why we needed the lantern,' said Archie, as he gingerly made his way into the tunnel. He waited for the others to follow him down the steps. 'We've used the bell, the map, the ring and the lantern. That just leaves the message on the piece of paper, and the hammer. We must be getting close to finding the treasure.'

There was no sign of the dragons anywhere. They walked at a swift pace, with Sherbet trotting a little in front. The tunnel seemed to go on for miles. The passage's walls were decorated with the same patterns as the fireplace, the light from the lantern reflecting off gems inlaid in the eyes of strange beasts or from the centres of flowers.

Sherbet barked from the darkness ahead of them. The dog appeared, running in terror. He hid behind Archie's ankles, staring back at the shadows.

'What's the matter, boy?' said Archie. He moved forward slowly, holding the lantern up high. An enormous face stared out at him from the blackness. All three children jumped back in fright, ready to run, but the face didn't move. It was carved from the rock, its features frozen into a forbidding expression. It filled the tunnel from floor to ceiling, creating a dead end. Cold eyes glared at the intruders.

'It's Gregor McBudge,' said Archie, recognising the face from the portrait room. 'He's my ancestor. He's supposed to have helped a dragon in the forest.'

'He doesn't look very friendly,' said Billy. A deep, unearthly voice, like the sound of wind whipping through sand, echoed from the face in answer.

'ONLY THOSE WHO REMEMBER MAY PASS,' it said. They trembled at the noise.

'He doesn't sound very friendly either!' Billy squeaked.

'Remember?' said Archie, quaking. 'Remember what?'

'What's left in the tool kit?' said Fliss. Archie opened the box. There was the hammer and the strange message still left unused. The hammer didn't feel right – he wasn't going to try and smash his ancestor in the face. He held the lantern over the paper.

MEMENTO MISERICORDIAE.
REMEMBER MERCY.

'We remember!' Archie yelled at the face. 'We remember mercy!' The face was silent.

'It's not working,' said Fliss. 'The message isn't getting through.'

'It's not a message,' Archie realised. 'It's a *password*.' He cleared his throat and said, '*Memento misericordiae.*'

There was a *clank* from behind the face, followed by a grinding sound. The face split into two at the mouth, the two halves sliding slowly into the rock in opposite directions so that the mouth opened wide. A golden, welcome glow poured into the tunnel from between the teeth, dazzling them after they had been in the dark for so long. Archie shielded his eyes with his hand and stepped into the mouth.

The first thing Archie noticed was the sweet aroma of
caramel that drifted around him.

'It smells like the McBudge factory in here,' said Fliss,
who was right behind him. 'Only ... better.'

'If that's possible,' said Billy, drinking in the air. Then
he gasped as, along with the others, his eyes adjusted to
the light. The spectacle in front of them made them stop
in their tracks and stare.

The tunnel had opened out on to an enormous cavern,
a cathedral carved out of the rock. Golden crystals – some
as large as tree trunks, others as small as toadstools –
sprouted from every surface; long, many-sided tubes
of shimmering, honeyed glass, just like the one that
caged the wyrdie-light inside Archie's lantern. The

gemstone-carpeted depths of the cave glittered in the reflected fires of hundreds of scattered torches, and everywhere the same sweet scent filled the air. A low humming, like the sound of a thousand beehives, echoed around the cavern. It was as if the whole place were singing.

The children stepped further into the cavern, following a path that wound through the forest of crystals. Billy nudged Archie's side.

'There are tree roots *everywhere*,' said the boy, pointing at the ground. The golden stones were interlaced with meandering plant fibres. 'This must be a major nexus for wyrdiness.'

Fliss stopped at one of the bigger crystals and laughed delightedly.

'The *dragons*!' she said. She waved them over. 'They live here – look!'

Archie and Billy peered into the stone. It wasn't solid like they expected, but hollow. Inside lay a sleeping creature. Fliss was right: they were no bigger than kittens. But it was definitely a dragon, its little wings wrapped around a scaly body, looking just like the stone dragons that guarded the roof of Honeystone Hall.

'Each big crystal has a dragon in it,' said Fliss, running

from one stone to the next and pressing her nose against
their polished surfaces. 'That humming you can hear –
it's their *snoring*.'

'There's one that hasn't gone to sleep,' said Archie. He
pointed to a little dragon that was still fluttering about
the cavern. It saw them, and swiftly flew over, landing in
Fliss's outstretched hand and squeaking a greeting.
Sherbet barked at it and received a short blast of dragon-
fire on the nose for his trouble.

'It's the dragon that stopped and looked at us in the

castle,' said Fliss. 'The one that was last. Look at its little feet – those fiery footprints in Clootie's café were left by a dragon, I'm sure. They're *so* adorable!'

'I bet they're not great as pets,' said Billy. 'Imagine that chasing the postman. Your letters would end up as toast.'

The dragon took off and flew along the path. Then it paused, hovering like a hummingbird and turning to look back at them with its big yellow eyes.

'It wants us to follow,' said Archie. The dragon led them down the pathway, keeping a little way ahead, until they were deep inside the cavern. It halted at a large cluster of crystals that had been arranged into an untidy circle. A voice, craggy and deep, bellowed from inside it.

'The McBudge heir has arrived. In spite of my eyesight, I'd recognise that face anywhere.'

Over the side of what they realised was a kind of nest, peered another dragon, larger than the others. It clambered unsteadily out on to the ground in front of them, its wrinkled hide shedding scales even as they watched. Its golden eyes were old and misted. The elderly creature coughed violently and spat a fireball past Billy's ear.

'It's the Tablet of dragons,' whispered Fliss.

'Welcome to the Cavern of Honeystone, McBudge,' the dragon said, squinting at Archie. 'You've the look of Gregor the Hairy about you. Though you need to work on the beard.'

'You knew Gregor McBudge?' said Archie, fascinated. This dragon must really be ancient!

'I'm Old Jings, the dragon he found injured in the forest. He looked after me and I learned your human tongue. We used to have a lot of dealings with humans long ago, but now we keep to ourselves. I'm the only dragon left in the Cavern of Honeystone that still knows the human speech.'

'Honeystone,' said Archie. 'Like Honeystone Hall!'

'This is the source of all the honeystone in the world,' said Old Jings, 'hidden in the roots of the mountain of Ben Doodle.'

Archie looked around at the crystals.

'What's it for?' he said. 'Do you dig it out of the ground?'

Old Jings wheezed merrily.

'You have much to learn, young McBudge,' it said. 'Honeystone is *made* by us, the honey dragons!'

'Honey dragons!' squealed Fliss. 'Like honey bees!'

'But with a serious wyrdie-upgrade,' said Billy.

'In the summer we fly around the heather up on the high moors, gathering nectar – yes, just like bees. But then *we* use our magical dragon-fire to turn the nectar into honeystone crystals. It is our food and our protection. Now, with the first snows, we're preparing to hibernate inside our honeystone cocoons, until spring comes once more. Except for that one,' the dragon pointed a bony claw at the little dragon that had sat itself on Fliss's shoulder. 'She's always the last to hibernate.'

'She's trying to stay awake,' said Fliss, scratching the little animal's chin. 'She thinks she'll miss out on something if she's asleep.' The little dragon opened its mouth wide and let out a huge yawn.

'Out of the mouth of the dragon!' said Archie, suddenly recalling the family motto. '*De Ore Draconis.* D.O.D. – this is the 'dod' Mum found out about. The honeystone is made from the fire that comes *out of the mouth of the dragon*. It's the secret ingredient – we've found it!'

33

Old Jings chuckled.

'Good to know there's a brain inside that soft little human body of yours,' he said. 'Now let's see if you can work out the last bit of the challenge.'

'We need to get the honeystone out of the cavern and back to Dundoodle,' said Archie, thinking hard. He opened the box. 'The hammer will break the crystals.'

'The hammer is made from draconium,' said Old Jings, as Archie lifted it from the box and admired its serpentine shape. 'The only substance in the world that can break honeystone. You know what you have to do, McBudge.'

Archie stepped over to one of the larger empty crystals that stood nearby.

'Stand back!' he said. The others watched as he swung the hammer back, then struck the crystal sharply with the metal dragon head. The stone rang like a bell before shattering into many smaller shards that spilled over the rocky ground.

'How do we get this home?' said Billy. 'We can't fill our pockets with rubble.'

'That's what the honeystone casket is for,' said Jings. 'You should have brought it with you.'

'The casket?' Archie said, a chill running down his spine. '*What casket?*'

'The honeystone casket,' the dragon repeated. 'Fashioned from the wood of the Wyrdie Tree. Spells of protection were woven into its making by the tree sprites of the old forest. Only a McBudge can open it.'

'Wow,' said Billy. 'That's in the super league of magical objects.'

'I – I don't have it!' stammered Archie. In his panic he thought back to Great-Uncle Archibald's letter – it said there were *six* clues, he was sure of it, and they had found *six* things. How could he have missed this? He looked at the others in alarm.

Then he touched the wooden box that had belonged to Dad. The only thing of Dad's he actually owned. It was just an ordinary, dull-looking, brown wood container that Dad had kept keys and coins in, but it was one of his most prized possessions.

'This … this is the casket, isn't it?' said Archie, his voice trembling. The dragon gave him a toothy smile. Archie stared at the box, his mind spinning and his heart ready to burst. Dad must have known about the Quest all along! That's why he'd given the box to Archie. *You may find help in the strangest ways*, the letter had said. In a fashion, Dad had been by his side for the whole of the Quest. He sniffed gratefully as he opened the casket.

'Tablet will show you how to grind up the honeystone into a powder for the fudge recipe,' said Old Jings, as Billy and Fliss helped Archie collect the shards and put them into the box. Tablet was in on the secret too! Archie had always suspected the butler knew more than he was saying. 'You've completed the test of the McBudges,' the dragon yawned. 'Well done! You may leave the cavern and return home.'

'But I've so many questions!' said Archie. The Quest was over but he felt like he was only just beginning to understand what it meant to be a McBudge. 'What about Gregor? He rescued you and was rewarded for his mercy, rewarded with honeystone. But there's more, isn't there? The *magic* – there's magic in the family. How?'

The dragon's head nodded sleepily.

'All will be revealed in time,' it said, before dozing off completely. A snore flapped from its mouth as it fell back into its crystal nest.

'But … but …' said Archie. He still didn't have all the answers.

'We'd better go,' said Billy. The little dragon had also disappeared.

The children quietly made their way back through the cavern, then up the dark tunnel, each lost in their own thoughts. Even Fliss was unusually silent, wrapping her coat tightly around her. They clambered out of the fire-place into the great hall. It was late afternoon and the sky was darkening. There was no sign of anyone. Billy produced the old map of the castle.

'I'll try and find us a quicker way back to the quayside,' he said. It was then that Archie remembered what he had been about to say when they were distracted by the arrival of the dragons.

'The name of the pupil who drew this plan,' he said. 'What was it?'

Billy squinted at the bottom of the map where a name had been scrawled with an inky pen.

'It says … Spotty Hanklecrumb?'

'Actually,' said a voice from the shadows. 'I think you'll find that's *Hankiecrust. Scotty* Hankiecrust, though my handwriting was always terrible.'

34

Even without the lantern, Archie would have known who the man was by the sniffing sound he made.

'Mr Hankiecrust,' he said. 'What are you doing here?' But he thought he knew the reason why.

The factory manager stepped out from the shadow of the castle wall where he had been concealed. The light from Archie's lantern reflected off his glasses as two yellow spots, hiding the man's eyes from them.

'Archie,' he said, smiling. 'And your friends too – my goodness! Out for a jolly adventure!' He walked towards them. 'But you shouldn't be out in such weather! Let me take you all home.'

'We're fine, thank you,' said Archie guardedly. It seemed such a strange thing to say, standing in the middle of an abandoned, haunted castle on a cold, snowy day. Things were not fine at all.

'What's that under your arm?' said Mr Hankiecrust, pointing at the box of honeystone. 'Is that the secret ingredient you have there?' His voice had an edge to it that made Archie afraid. 'I should have known old McBudge kept it hidden away at Pookiecrag. You'd better give it to me for safekeeping.'

'No, thank you,' said Archie, nervously backing away.

'Come along, Archie,' said Mr Hankiecrust, taking another step forward. 'We haven't got all day. I've been wandering blindly around in the mist in this miserable ruin all afternoon. I've no time for your nonsense!'

'I'd rather not …' began Archie.

'Give it to me, you stupid boy!' snapped Mr Hankiecrust.

He suddenly lunged to seize the box. Fliss gave a shout of warning. But Archie was too quick for the man and ducked, throwing the box to Billy who was already halfway out of the hall. Billy caught it and ran down the passageway towards the loch. Sherbet, barking furiously, launched himself at Mr Hankiecrust who fell backwards in surprise, not having noticed the white dog against the snow-dappled ground. The

man's feet slipped on the icy flagstones and he landed
heavily, bumping his head and letting out a curse. By the
time he'd scrambled back up, Archie and Fliss were
running for the boat, with the fearless little dog on their
heels.

Billy was waiting for them at the quay. In their haste
they half jumped, half fell into their boat. It rocked violently then immediately lurched from its mooring, as if it
sensed their urgency. They looked back to see the man
running angrily along the quayside in pursuit. But Mr
Hankiecrust could only watch and rub his bruises as the

dragon boat sped away from the castle across the black water of the loch.

'That was close!' said Archie, catching his breath. He hugged Sherbet tightly to him, never more grateful for the dog than now. 'Good boy, Sherbet!'

'What happened to Mrs Puddingham-Pye?' said Billy. 'Are she and Mr Hankiecrust *both* after the secret ingredient?'

'He must want it for himself,' said Archie, frowning at the box of honeystone. 'Or maybe to sell to someone like Mrs Puddingham-Pye. It's that valuable.'

'He saw us with the toffee jigsaw,' remembered Billy. 'And must have recognised the plan of the castle from when he was at school. He guessed the jigsaw was left there by your great-uncle to lead you to the honeystone.'

'Then to get the map he trashed the hideout,' said Fliss heatedly. 'He probably used that when he was a kid too.'

Archie nodded but he was confused: why *hadn't* Mrs Puddingham-Pye been at the castle? He wasn't disappointed, but with everything she knew about the Quest and its magical nature, surely she must have known about Pookiecrag and the honey dragons? Was she working with Mr Hankiecrust? He still felt like he didn't have all the answers.

They heard the sound of a boat's engine some way behind them. Mr Hankiecrust was chasing after them. He'd soon catch up! Even through the mist they could see he had a grim look on his face, not like the friendly factory manager they thought they knew.

The boat steered itself back into the cave under the house and came to rest on the beach. They jumped out, then slipped and stumbled up the steps of the tunnel and burst into the library. The fire had gone out and the room was dark. If Mr Hankiecrust was following he would have seen where their boat had gone and couldn't be far behind them.

'Hide!' said Archie. Fliss jumped behind the curtain, whilst Billy tried to make himself look like a lamp-stand before ducking behind an armchair with Sherbet. Archie dived under the desk with the box. They could hear Mr Hankiecrust's deliberate footsteps, one after another, as he slowly and cautiously climbed the stairs of the tunnel. There was a creak as he pushed the book-case open.

'I know you're in here, children,' he said, stepping into

the room with a sniff. 'And sooner or later I'm going to find you ...'

35

Mr Hankiecrust crept towards the desk. *He's seen me*, thought Archie. But there was a rustle from the window and the man turned around sharply.

'I spy someone hiding,' sang Mr Hankiecrust, as he tiptoed across the floor in the direction of the curtains. He was going to find Fliss!

Archie scrambled to his feet and threw himself at the man.

'You stupid little wretch!' said Mr Hankiecrust, grabbing him roughly by the shoulders and gripping him tightly so that he couldn't move. 'That was your last mistake! You should never have come here!'

'Let me go!' cried Archie, but the grip only tightened. Fliss jumped out from behind the curtain.

'Eat fiery doom, you snivelling hideout wrecker!' cried Fliss. A ball of flames launched itself from inside her coat, whizzing around Hankiecrust's head, the sudden light dazzling him.

It was the little honey dragon! Fliss must have been hiding it in her coat all along.

'What is it?' yelled Hankiecrust, trying to swat the creature away, but he still kept one hand firmly on Archie's shoulder.

Then, out of the corner of Archie's eye, he saw a spark fall from the painting of his great-uncle, landing in the fireplace. With a roar the fire erupted into life, the flames sending flickering shadows writhing over the walls of the library. A great gust of air rushed down the chimney, blasting out of the hearth and screaming in circles around the room. A shuddering, smoking shape formed in front of them from the fire and ash and dust. In his head, Archie made a list of words he would use to describe a ghost and ticked them all off: the shape was Great-Uncle Archibald and he was *not happy*.

'HANKIECRUST!' bellowed the apparition.

'Mr McBudge!' squealed the man. 'But you're meant to be d-d-dead!'

'Scotty Hankiecrust, you horrible little *worm*!' said the

ghost. 'I *am* dead.' Mr Hankiecrust yelped and fell back into the armchair, dropping Archie and knocking over Billy, who was crouched behind the chair with Sherbet. 'I trusted you,' continued Great-Uncle Archibald, 'and *this* is how you repay me!'

Mr Hankiecrust shivered and whimpered. The children stared at the ghost, half in fear and half in amazement.

'Don't hurt me!' the man pleaded. 'I needed the secret ingredient.' He began to babble miserably. 'I had no choice, don't you see? I'd borrowed money from the McBudge bank account – all of it – and I thought I could repay it by selling the secret ingredient to someone else, another company.'

'Like the Puddingham-Pye Cookie Company perhaps?' came a snarl from the library doorway. Mrs Puddingham-Pye sauntered into the room. She looked around menacingly – she didn't seem surprised to see the ghost, but Archie could see a fearful respect in her face. She opened her handbag and Garstigan crawled out, hopping on to the shoulder of her long black coat like some kind of gruesome adornment. The little monster eyed the hovering honey dragon with suspicion.

'Come to rescue your accomplice?' snapped Archie.

'Snotty Hankiecrust? He's nothing to do with me, Urchin,' she said, throwing a distasteful glance at the trembling man in the chair. 'Dear *late* Great-Uncle Archibald summoned me.'

'What?' said Archie. He turned to the ghost, astonished. 'She's tried to stop me finding the honeystone. Her kids have tried to *kill* me!'

'Darling Georgie and Portia do so enjoy their little *hobbies*,' said Mrs Puddingham-Pye fondly. 'Such *creative* children.'

'I *did* summon her,' admitted Great-Uncle Archibald. He looked at the boy kindly. 'I need her here, Archie. I need her here so I can tell you the *truth*.'

36

'She was never after the honeystone, was she?' said Archie.

Mrs Puddingham-Pye arched an eyebrow but said nothing. The ghost smiled.

'You're the canny boy I thought you were,' it said. 'Just like your father. And you'll need to be, as the heir of the McBudges.

'You see, the McBudge family have not always made sweets and fudge. Hundreds of years ago, the clan McBudge were tasked with being the Guardians of the Wyrdie Tree. They were bound to safeguard its magic, the source of all the magic in Dundoodle, from evil intent.

'The chief of the clan was gifted with the ability to *wyrdwork* – casting spells, summoning the hidden folk of the forest, talking with the spirits of the trees. That gift was inherited by the chief's heir on completion of a test, and so passed down through the generations.'

Archie's mouth was dry. He would inherit *magic powers*? Everyone in the room was watching him, except Billy who was scribbling down the ghost's every word in his book. Archie could see he would have his very own chapter and Macabre Creepy Scale rating. The ghost continued.

'When an enterprising McBudge discovered that honeystone could be used to make sweets, the family built the factory and moved to this house in Dundoodle instead, leaving Pookiecrag Castle to the dragons. The legend of its haunting was meant to keep people away and protect its secrets.'

Great-Uncle Archibald drifted over to Mrs Puddingham-Pye and looked straight into her face. She flinched and Garstigan hissed uneasily.

'I've summoned you here to inform you that Archie has passed the test,' said the ghost. 'Thus he is the true heir and is now the Guardian.'

'She was trying to stop you passing the test, Archie,' said Fliss. 'We thought she was after the honeystone, but it was just a smokescreen. She wanted you to fail the test, as that would make *her* the next candidate for heir.'

'That's if the Piglets didn't finish me off first,' said
Archie. He glared at the woman. 'But you've *already* got
magical powers.'

'Everyone in the family has potential,' said Mrs
Puddingham-Pye, tickling Garstigan's belly so that he
purred. 'It's in the blood. But the real power lies with the
chief of the clan.' She laughed nastily. 'You've no idea
what you're dealing with, you little scrap!'

Archie clenched his fists but his great-uncle's ghost
waved a hand dismissively.

'In every chocolate box there's that odd chocolate

that no one really likes,' it said. 'And so it is with every generation of McBudges. There's always a bad'un. But, Archie, you're now officially the chief. And she'll respect that.'

The woman leaned towards Archie, just like she had on the first day they'd met.

'For now,' she whispered in his ear.

'This is mad! You're all mad!' It was Mr Hankiecrust. 'Ghosts and goblins and weirdos! I'm imagining things – it's not happening!' They'd forgotten all about him, cowering in the chair. Before anyone had a chance to move, he leaped up and sprinted out of the library, frantically hurrying for the front door. Archie ran to the window in time to see Mr Hankiecrust scurry down the steps, then suddenly fall to the ground, hit on the head by a stone dragon that for some reason had chosen that moment to fall from the roof.

'I think the twins might have been busy outside,' remarked Mrs Puddingham-Pye, joining him at the window. 'I do believe their aim is improving.'

Archie lay on the sofa in the library with Sherbet asleep on his lap. The fire gently crackled, unlike the alarming performance of the previous afternoon. *It has been a good day*, he thought. A busy day.

Tablet had shown him how to grind up the honeystone crystals with a draconium pestle and mortar for use in the McBudge Fudge recipe, so fudge was being made in the factory again. Archie had taken a sample of the first batch to test. It very much met with his approval. It turned out Tablet was half-gnome and had worked for the McBudges for centuries.

'I'm older than I look, you know,' he wheezed, which didn't actually seem possible.

The Puddingham-Pyes were keeping a low profile, a

temporary truce having been declared now that all the secrets were out in the open. If they ever caused trouble again … well, Archie would be ready. His *wyrdworker* powers might take years to develop, he had been told, but he wasn't in any hurry. He'd had quite enough of magic. For a little while, at least.

Mr Hankiecrust had woken up that morning in hospital with a very bad headache. The bump on the head also appeared to have given him amnesia. He couldn't even remember that he was the McBudge factory manager. He had decided to leave Dundoodle for good and start a new life elsewhere. Archie would never find out what the man had spent all his great-uncle's money on, but it didn't matter as the business was saved. He and Mum could live on happily in the Hall after all, even if they weren't as rich as everyone thought they were.

Archie had been very pleased to give the job of factory manager to Mr Hankiecrust's assistant (who just happened to be Fliss's dad). Fliss was overjoyed that she had been able to help her dad out and had bought Archie an extra-large piece of fudge cake from Clootie Dumpling's as a 'thank you'.

'I suppose you've earned it,' she said with a grin. 'I

reckon you do deserve to live here after everything that's happened.'

The little honey dragon, which had *accidentally* fallen into Fliss's coat, had been named Blossom. She made a home for herself in the greenhouse, which had plenty of flowers to keep her in nectar through the winter. She had already made a nest in a palm tree, and only occasionally set fire to things.

Billy had so much new information for his *Book of Wyrdiness of Dundoodle and its Surroundings* that he would be busy for ages. He had assigned Archie a Macabre Creepy Scale rating of only four point three.

'Temporarily,' he said. 'I'll reconsider once you've done some *proper* magic. Extra points for anything involving the undead.'

Mum had stopped worrying (for now). She knew nothing about what had happened, and Archie thought it was better that way, though he wasn't quite sure she believed his story about finding the 'dod' in the attic of Honeystone Hall. He could hear her busily decorating a Christmas tree in the hallway with Tablet's help. It looked like it was going to be the best Christmas in a long time.

He looked up at the portrait of his great-uncle. The old man's face winked at him.

'What happens now?' said Archie, smiling. 'Are you going to stick around now that your job is done, Great-Uncle?'

'Perhaps,' said the painting. 'Just to see how you get on.'

Sherbet opened one eye and wagged his tail at his ghostly old master. Archie looked thoughtfully at the wooden box, the honeystone casket, in its new home on the mantelpiece.

'Is everyone who dies a ghost?' he asked after a pause. 'Is my dad a ghost?'

The portrait's features softened.

'If he is, I've not seen him around,' it said. 'But don't worry. That means he's probably at peace. And why wouldn't he be? Knowing he has a son like you.'

Archie smiled and helped himself to another piece of fudge.

'That's good,' he said happily. It was one more good thing to add to a very long list.

Acknowledgements

Thank you to Francesca Mancuso for Latin help. Also, thanks to the team at Bloomsbury who made this book become a reality. Although my name is on the cover, many people have been busy helping behind the scenes – from editorial and design to marketing and sales – and I'm extremely grateful to all of them. Finally, thank you to Claire Powell, whose illustrations brought Dundoodle magically to life.

ARCHIE, FLISS, BILLY and SHERBET

will be back in the next book in

THE DUNDOODLE MYSTERIES

COMING 2019